AFTER DEATH DO US PART

SARA-LISA ANDERSSON

THE ROAD up the coast was winding and narrow and at times came so close to the angry waves pounding at the cliffs below that it made my stomach clench with every spurt of foam.

"Could you please tell me where we're going?" I pleaded for the fourth or fifth time, but my husband just smiled.

I turned my head and tried to focus on the road ahead. I'd never been up this way before, not this far, at least. We'd been driving for almost an hour, and it had been ages since I'd seen anything that looked even remotely familiar. The road signs were few and far apart, and the names on them didn't provide any clues as to where we were going. I tried to keep my eyes on the furthest part of the road, to dampen the nausea, and eventually the carsickness subsided slightly, but the ominous feeling I got from Thomas's secretive smile refused to abate.

After another ten miles or so, Thomas finally slowed down and turned off from the main road. I sat up and looked around. Was this our destination? I couldn't see anything that would explain why Thomas had been acting so weird lately. Just a smaller, equally winding road leading up to an old and rather dilapidated house that looked like something out of a horror movie. It hadn't been painted in decades, and the salty wind from the sea had made it anyone's guess what color it had originally been. Now it was a dingy gray, and the windows were like black empty eye sockets staring right at me. Not exactly a welcoming sight. It was a good thing I didn't spook easily.

"Is this where we're going?" I looked at Thomas again. He still didn't reply, but his smile had turned into a grin that made my skin crawl. I hadn't seen him this excited in ages, but instead of making me curious, it filled me with dread. What was going on?

Thomas drove up to the house, parked right in front of the large porch and stepped out. He walked around the car and opened my door, offering his arm to help me get out. He had always had an air of old-fashioned chivalry about him. That had been one of the things that attracted me to him when we first met, more than ten years ago now. Many of the things that had seemed charming or endearing back then no longer had the same effect on me.

I stepped out of the car without taking his offered arm, pulled my coat tight around me to keep the relentless wind out, and looked at him with a frown. "Thomas. Honestly. Could you please tell me what we're doing here?"

Thomas smiled from ear to ear, stepped back and reached out his arm toward the house in a dramatic gesture. "Ta-ra!" he said triumphantly and bowed like a circus ringmaster presenting someone doing something spectacular on a tightrope.

I stared at him, at the house, and then at Thomas again. "Ta-ra?" I felt my heart sink. Oh no. Please no.

"Isn't it great, Lisa?" Thomas bounded up the steps to the porch like an eager puppy. "Isn't it just amazing? Don't you just love it?"

I stared at the peeling facade, the rotted porch, the black, empty windows and the bleak surroundings. There was no one around for miles and miles. We had passed a small house just after turning off from the main road, and I thought that I could make out part of the roof down there behind the trees, and a thin wisp of smoke from the chimney. Although the road up here had taken a winding detour, it was still a pretty long hike as the crow flies, all the way on the other side of a large pasture. With cows in it! Might as well be on the other side of the moon.

"What did you do?" I whispered, and turned toward Thomas again. He didn't hear me, as he was busy fiddling with the lock on the front door. He gave the door a firm push with his shoulder, and it opened with a wooden groan. "Thomas?" I tried again, louder this time, but my voice didn't carry in the gusty wind, and Thomas had already disappeared into the cavernous house.

I carefully climbed the steps to the porch and walked over to the front door. "Thomas?"

It was dark inside, and I couldn't see a thing when I first stepped into the hallway. A strong scent of damp and mold made me lift my arm to cover my mouth. No one could have lived here for years. Perhaps even decades. "Thomas?"

"Isn't it great!" he exclaimed and popped up out of nowhere from behind the door. I jumped and put one hand over my heart.

"Don't do that!" I shrieked, but Thomas just laughed.

"Isn't it amazing?" he said and continued into a room on the left. I followed him.

"Thomas. Could you please tell me …?"

He stopped and turned right in the middle of the large front room. "It's ours. Isn't it just great?"

I stared at him. "What do you mean, *ours?*"

He walked over to me and took me in his arms. "Ours, as in yours and mine," he said and leaned in to kiss me.

I pushed him away. "What do you mean, yours and mine? Please tell me you didn't …"

He smiled proudly. "I bought it. You and I are officially in escrow, baby. Can you believe it? Homeowners? You and me?"

My entire body went completely cold. "Thomas. What did you do?"

He kept walking into a room toward the back, and I followed him. This room must have a view of the gray and angry ocean pounding against the cliffs just behind the house but I could barely see it through the grimy windows. "Thomas?"

He reached out his arms and smiled at me, just brimming with enthusiasm. "Just look at this. All of this is ours. Isn't it great?" Without waiting for a reply, he turned his back on me and kept walking into yet another room.

I almost had to run to keep up with him, and could feel my chest tighten as the meaning of his words started to sink in. "Thomas, please tell me that you didn't …"

"We got a great deal," he said but didn't look at me. "The price per square foot was ridiculous."

But there were a lot of square feet. The rooms seemed to multiply as Thomas kept walking through the dilapidated old building.

"Thomas," I pleaded, and the confusion I'd felt started to give way to full-blown panic.

We had come full circle and were back in the hallway inside the front door where a wide and rather steep staircase led up to a landing where the stairs turned 90 degrees before continuing up to the second floor. Thomas bounded up the stairs, completely oblivious to the ominous creaks in the old and withered wood.

When I caught up with him, he was standing in a large room at the back of the house, also with a sea view somewhere behind the grime. There was a tiled stove in the corner and a faded patterned wallpaper on the walls. It had probably been a beautiful room, once. A long, long time ago. "Thomas, please," I pleaded again, and he turned toward me.

"What is the matter with you, Lisa?" he said. "Why aren't you excited? Isn't this the greatest house you've ever seen?"

I shook my head. "Thomas, how did you pay for it?" I held my breath waiting for the answer.

"Just a small mortgage," he said and held out his arms. "The payments will be negligible since we were able to make such a large down payment."

There it was. My fear manifested itself as freezing claws along my spine.

"Thomas," I said, and there was an edge to my voice. "What did you do, Thomas? What did you do with my money?"

"*Our* money, sweetheart." Thomas sounded slightly annoyed. "The real estate agent said that this was an excellent investment. Once we have fixed this house up a little, it's going to be worth twice what we paid for it. Maybe even more."

"But that money…"

"Yes?"

"That money was for …"

"For our future, sweetheart. Wasn't that what your grandmother said?"

"Yes, but she didn't mean …"

"What could have been a better way of spending that money? You tell me. This is an investment of a lifetime."

"I thought that we were going to try …"

"Try what, sweetheart? This is going to be great, you wait and see."

"Well … I thought, perhaps, IVF …"

Thomas abruptly turned his back and walked away before I could finish the sentence. I followed him out the door. The landing was dark and narrow with doors leading in all directions, room after room after room, like something out of a nightmare, a place to get lost in and never find one's way out of again. I had a feeling that my nightmare was just beginning.

He disappeared into one of the rooms, and I followed him into what turned out to be a large bathroom with a lion claw tub and flowered tiles on the walls. It was elegant in an ancient and dilapidated way.

"Could we please … talk about this?" My voice

echoed against the hard tiles, and I lowered my voice half way through the sentence.

He stood with his back to me, staring at the wall as if he was studying the pipes and fittings to the bath, but the back of his neck looked angry and tense, and I didn't think that he was that interested in plumbing. It was weird, but I knew what his face looked like even though he was facing the other way. We had been married more than ten years. I knew him by now.

"Thomas, please."

He turned toward me abruptly. "There's nothing to talk about. The decision has been made. The contracts are signed. The house is bought. We are going to make a bundle on this, and then we can use that money for our next venture. This is the beginning of something great, trust me. I know what I'm doing."

He walked straight past me out onto the landing and down the stairs. I sat down on the edge of the tub and stared at the dusty tiles.

For some reason, I didn't believe him.

2

THOMAS'S PLANS TO double my inheritance stalled almost straight out of the gate when it turned out to be difficult to find a contractor who was prepared to work on the renovations. Several of the people he called refused to even come out and look at the property, once they heard which house it was, and the ones that did come by soon departed when they heard what Thomas was willing to pay for the work.

Every night he sat at the small kitchen table in our apartment with his computer and his spread sheets, a deep frown on his forehead, growing more and more frustrated with every phone call or email.

When it came time to pay the bills, he sat for a long time, staring at the rent and utilities. Then he turned toward me where I stood at the sink.

"We're just going to have to move in."

"What? To the house? But—"

"There's no point in paying rent for this tiny apartment when we've got a great big house just standing there, waiting for us."

"But that house …" I shook my head and felt the tight knot in my stomach tighten even harder. When Thomas had his mind set on something, there usually wasn't much I could do. "There's so much that needs to be done before anyone could ever live there."

He brushed off my objections. "It will be so much easier to deal with all of this if we're living on site. It's been murder having to drive back and forth for all the meetings with those lousy contractors." He glanced at the stack of bills next to him on the table. "I'll call the landlord in the morning and see if we can get out of the lease by the end of the month. I'm sure we can work something out."

I just stared at him. "You mean … move in two weeks?"

"Yeah," he said and pulled his computer closer to start up a new spreadsheet to plan the move. "The sooner the better."

I wanted to say no, really, I did. I wanted to scream and yell and demand to get my money back, *my* money that I'd inherited from *my* grandmother that had been intended to use for IVF, not for some wild house flipping scheme. I wanted to put my foot down, give him an ultimatum, make a stand, demand that he listened to me and that he didn't just make decisions like these without even consulting me.

Instead I turned back toward the dishes, plunging my hands into the water that was so hot that my skin turned bright red. It hurt, but the pain was nothing compared to the agony that tore me apart. It was too late. The money was gone. There was nothing I could do about it. There would never be any children. I would never be a mom.

And if that dream, the only one I'd ever had, couldn't ever come true, then …

Then there really wasn't anything worth getting into a fight with Thomas about.

I didn't really care anymore.

3

I DROPPED the brush in the bucket and sat back on my heels, massaging my lower back. The large reception room overlooking the sea was still empty, but now it was at least clean. Oh, so very clean. It had taken several days just to get the kitchen, the bathroom, and the master bedroom upstairs suitable for habitation, and now that we had moved in, I still had the rest of the house to sort out. I sighed and looked around at the big, empty space. I'd put in hours of work, and it showed, but I still didn't feel the least bit good about the result of my efforts.

This room would be our living room, and perhaps this would be where we would entertain our guests. As soon as I had pictured it—the two sofas opposite each other over by the large fireplace, the gleaming chandelier hanging from the ceiling, soft chiming music in the background and enticing smells coming from the large kitchen a couple of rooms down—I pushed the image aside. There was no money left of my inheritance for decorating, and there would be no entertaining, I could be sure of that. Thomas didn't care much for socializing, and anyway, there was no one around here to socialize with, even if we had wanted to. I still hadn't met the distant neighbors on the other side of the cow pasture but was already quite certain that Thomas would find some reason to dislike them, just as he had done with our neighbors back in town, and all my old friends and co-workers that I had slowly lost touch with over the past ten years.

I carried the bucket to the utility room by the back door and emptied it, wringing the rag and placing the bristle brush on the side of the vast sink to dry. I washed my hands—red and prune-like from all the scrubbing—and wiped them on my jeans as I walked back out into the hallway, as always adding things that needed to be cleaned, painted, mended, replaced to my mental To-do-list. There was so much to do.

Thomas's enthusiasm over the house had faded as quickly as it had come over him, as soon as his plans for a quick renovation and an equally quick buck had failed. None of the local contractors had been willing to take on the work, and when he'd run out of people to call, he'd just torn up his plans and given up. I'd suggested that we could do some of the work ourselves, and just get professionals in for things like the plumbing and the electric, but he'd just brushed me off, muttering something about the reason he went to university was so that he didn't have to do manual labor.

When he came home from work in the evenings, he just ate his dinner and then went upstairs to the bedroom where he lay on the bed and watched TV until bedtime. I had tried to get him to help with some of the tasks that required his sinewy strength, but he kept putting it off, complaining that I never gave him a moment's peace. In the end, it was easier just to do it all myself.

After all, I had plenty of time to do it in. Thomas had decided that it would be pointless to get a second car just so that I could drive to my part-time job at the florist where I had been working for the last two years. My modest salary would barely cover the gas, he had pointed out, and I couldn't argue with that. My degree in French literature with a minor in philosophy hadn't turned out to be the best basis to build a lucrative career on, not that a career had ever been a part of my life plan. Instead, I'd had a series of part-time jobs over the years, just to get out of the house for a while, meet some people and make a little money. They had all been intended as a temporary measure, just something to keep myself occupied as I waited for my *real* life to begin. I'd never thought that I'd miss working when it came time to give it up, but I guess that those few hours of human interaction and light conversation with customers had meant more to me than I'd realized. But then I'd always expected that I'd stop working because I had something better to do with my time. Scrubbing floors wasn't exactly what I'd had in mind.

I had always planned on having children and becoming a housewife, and Thomas had been on board with that plan from the start. He was very career minded and seemed to like the idea of a wife that was always there for him and not off on her own business trips. For as long as I could remember it had been a dream of mine to be a stay-at-home mom and a homemaker and Thomas didn't seem to understand why I wasn't over the moon now, when I had a home and got to stay in it all day, every day. I hadn't been able to make him understand that this endless list of chores was not exactly what I had been dreaming of since I was a little girl, putting all my dolls properly to bed each night after feeding them and reading to them.

Thomas's long commute to work made my days go from dawn to dusk in complete solitude. The house was still mostly empty—our few belongings had barely taken up any space in the many cavernous rooms—and it sometimes gave me the creeps, but the spooky, haunted feeling that came from spider webs and dark corners everywhere I turned was nothing compared to the dread I felt, knowing that this money pit was the reason I would never have children. Never even have the chance to try, that is, since there were no guarantees with IVF.

I walked over to the window in the living room and looked out over the sea. It hadn't been calm since we'd moved here and I was starting to wonder if it ever would be. The choppy gray waves made me seasick even though the floorboards underneath my feet were made from solid oak. I turned away from the view and walked through all the rooms on the first floor. There was still so much to do, but my aching back told me that no more floors would be scrubbed today. The dining room would have to wait until tomorrow. But what should I do with the rest of the day? Thomas wouldn't be home for hours, and it wasn't time to start dinner yet.

I went up the still creaking but now at least dirt-free stairs to the second floor, but instead of surveying all the empty rooms there and making a list of what should be done, as I'd originally planned, I found myself walking over to the door at the far end of the landing. I had tried it before and knew it was locked, but last night when I was looking for the potato peeler, I'd found some keys in a kitchen drawer. Perhaps one of them would work.

The rusty, heavy key that I had hoped would fit was way too big for the keyhole, but one of the smaller ones slid right in, and despite the grime covering both door and handle, the lock turned easily and the door opened with just a small tug.

Inside was a narrow staircase, leading straight up into darkness. I looked around for a light switch but couldn't find one. Instead, I went into the master bedroom to get the large and heavy flashlight I kept on my nightstand because the light in the walk-in closet was broken. When I came back out into the hallway and switched it on, I saw that the staircase was covered in dust. It was evident that no one had been up here for decades, apart from the spiders. I shuddered and thought about just locking the door again, but in the end, curiosity got the better of me and I cautiously walked up the stairs. At the top, behind a railing to the left, was an enormous attic space, stretching the entire length and width of the house. It wasn't entirely dark since there were a couple of small windows at each end, but the thick layers of dust and grime kept most of the daylight out. I walked over to the closest window and managed to force it open. The gust of sea air was freezing against my face, but I preferred the cold to the stifling dust and smell of decay and closed-off spaces.

The light from the open window was enough to let

me switch off the flashlight, and I put it down on top of a box by the stairs. Unlike the rest of the house that had been completely empty when we moved in, the attic was filled with things, big and small, piles of boxes and crates and mysterious shapes covered in dust cloths. I walked over to the closest one and pulled the heavy sheet toward me, covering my nose and mouth with my arm as a cloud of dust rose in the still air. When the dust had begun to settle, I realized that I was looking at a small writing desk with a roll-up top. I gently eased it open and stared at the beautiful piece of furniture. It was magnificent. Probably an antique. There were two small drawers on either side and a shelf in the middle for stationary and whatever else ladies had wanted to keep close at hand a hundred years ago. Not their cell phones, obviously, even though the space would work perfectly as a charging station.

I reached for one of the little drawers, but just as I grabbed the small handle, the window behind me slammed shut, and I almost jumped out of my skin. A part of me wanted to just run back down the stairs, to the cold but bright and clean rooms downstairs, but I forced myself to get a grip, walked over to the window and pushed it open once more, this time securing it with the latch before I walked back and started examining my discovery.

A thorough inspection revealed nothing in the drawers and absolutely no flaws, and so I ignored my aching back and carried the small desk down to our bedroom on the second floor. The narrow space between the windows overlooking the sea seemed to have been made for this desk, but as soon as I'd thought that, I realized that it must be the other way around; the desk could actually have been made for this space. This was not IKEA stuff. It might very well have been made especially for someone who had lived here and wanted a writing desk to put in just this space. It looked so right there, as if it had never left that spot.

4

I WALKED BACK UP to the attic. Under the next dust cloth, I found several chairs, including one that looked like it would go perfectly with the small desk. A little further in, I found a sideboard that would be perfect for the dining room, once I'd scrubbed that floor, and a complete dining room set with eight wonderful chairs with tall, ornate backs. I didn't bother carrying anything else downstairs, just lifted dust cloths here and there and discovered enough side tables and lamps for all the rooms in the house, bed frames, armchairs, shelves and bureaus. There were also paintings in all sizes, both plain and ostentatious in wide, ornate frames. One of the smaller ones was particularly fetching—a watercolor of a small hillside village with chalk white houses with terracotta roofs overlooking an azure lake in the south of France or perhaps Italy, a very simple little piece of art made with just a few brush strokes in only a few distinct colors, but it looked just like I'd always imagined the Mediterranean, and since I'd always wanted to go there, I decided to hang it over my bed.

Rolled up in a corner, I found what appeared to be an oriental rug and after almost killing myself trying to maneuver the long and cumbersome shape down two sets of stairs, the carpet found its perfect place on the newly scrubbed floor in the living room where its soft pastel colors more than made up for the dreary gray ocean outside. It truly brightened the space, and I stood in the doorway afterward, wiping the dust and sweat from my forehead, smiling at the sight of my living room. It was such a small thing to be excited about, but it had been such a long time since I'd had a pleasant surprise that I intensely wanted to cherish it.

Almost giddy with excitement, I ran back up the stairs in search of more hidden treasures but stopped abruptly when I heard a car door slam shut. I turned and stared at the front door, and then hurried down to the bedroom to check the time on the alarm clock on Thomas's nightstand. Almost 7 PM. Thomas was home. And I hadn't even started dinner. Hadn't even thought about what I was going to make. My stomach growled, and I realized that I was starving. In all the excitement, I'd forgotten to eat lunch. Not that Thomas was going to care about that.

I hurried down the stairs and just barely made it out into the kitchen before the front door opened. A quick glance in the refrigerator revealed absolutely nothing that wouldn't take forever to prepare. I bit my lip and walked out into the hallway, bracing myself for the annoyance or perhaps even anger over not getting his dinner on time. He'd been in a foul mood since his big plans for the house fell through, and I'd been walking on egg shells over the last few weeks.

Thomas was pulling off his jacket, mail between his

teeth. His briefcase and a white plastic bag stood on the floor. I hurried over, took the envelopes from his mouth and kissed him. "Oh, hi. I'm so sorry, I completely lost track of time; I wasn't …"

But Thomas interrupted me. "Whatever you've made for dinner, just put it aside for another day. I suddenly had this craving for Chinese, and I drove past that place we used to go to. Do you remember?"

I breathed a sigh of relief. Sometimes, my husband's sudden impulses and mood swings were a pleasant surprise. I smiled at him. "Where that old man always used to sit in the corner, telling us stories in Cantonese?"

He nodded. "That's right. He was very eloquent. Too bad no one could understand a word he said."

I picked up the bag from the floor. "Well, he got to tell the stories," I said. "Sometimes that might just be enough. But you're never going to believe what I found in the attic. Come and see this." I walked through the front room, over to the door to the living room and pointed at the floor. "I'll just go and put this in some serving bowls and set the …"

Thomas grabbed hold of my waist and pulled me closer. "Wow, that is some rug!" He looked at me and smiled. "Don't bother setting the table. We have a perfect place for a picnic right here." He kissed me intensely and then pushed the hair out of my face. "I'm starving. Let's just christen the new rug." He winked at me, mischievously. "And then we really must eat, because as I said, I'm famished."

He kissed me again, and his hands searched eagerly for gaps in my clothing where he could get at my naked skin. Despite my hunger—intensified by the alluring smells coming from the bag I was holding—I felt a stronger urge well up inside of me, and the plastic bag fell to the floor as I grabbed my husband's shirt.

The carpet was soft and smooth, and as my clothes came off and I lay back on the floor, it almost felt as if it was caressing me at the same time Thomas was. It felt good to have him so close after all those lonely hours, but I couldn't help feeling vulnerable as I lay there, completely bare. Perhaps it was the large, curtain-less windows, perhaps the chilly air surrounding me or the emptiness of the vast room, but I'd never felt so exposed. The tingling of my skin was not solely caused by Thomas's wandering hands; it really felt as if there was someone watching us and I kept glancing over toward the doors to the front room and into the dining room, expecting to see someone standing there. But of course, there was no one but us in the house. We were miles away from another living soul. One good thing about not having any neighbors close by: you could have a quickie right on the living room floor without being caught. I could feel Thomas's urgent desire and hear him mumbling next to my ear as I pulled him even closer and tried to fill the void inside my soul with a few intense moments of physical pleasure. It didn't work, of course. It never did.

Soon he rolled off me, and I lay there, staring at the ceiling above. That would also need to be cleaned, perhaps even painted. But not tonight. I felt the stickiness between my thighs and the intense sadness that came over me every time, knowing that nothing would come of this, no matter how intense his desire for me was, or how much my body hungered after something to fill it up so completely that new life was created.

After more than ten years, I knew I wouldn't get pregnant. And I also knew that my husband wasn't as sad about that fact as I was.

As if he'd read my mind but gotten the message completely wrong, Thomas sighed contentedly. "It's so great that it's just you and me. Can you imagine having the house filled with kids, never ever getting a moment to ourselves?" He reached over me for the bag of Chinese food but couldn't reach it. "Hand me that, I'm starving."

I blinked the tears out of my eyes and gave him the bag before my growling stomach embarrassed me. Or my tears. Or something I might say.

The sweet and sour pork was just as good as I remembered it. Eating it right there on the soft, luxurious carpet, dressed only in my husband's discarded and wrinkled shirt, felt pretty nice, as well. There were some things I quite liked about being a homeowner.

But I would swap it all for a house full of kids, in a second.

5

THE NEXT MORNING, after Thomas had left for work, I went back out to the utility room and filled my bucket with hot water and pine-scented soap. The dining room was not as vast as the living room, but it still took several hours to clean, scrub and rid it of cobwebs. The arduous work felt a little easier today though, now that I knew that I had some furniture to decorate the room with when I was done. I couldn't wait to see the table and chairs back in their rightful place. The monster of a house had taken on a slightly different feel, and it almost felt as if I had been given a huge doll house as a present, with all the furniture packed away in a separate box. The idea of restoring the house to its former glory was energizing me, somehow. It wasn't my dream, but at least it was something to do. And I so desperately needed something to distract me. The solitude and isolation was starting to get on my nerves. A week or two spent mostly on my own could perhaps be seen as a retreat of sorts, a way to work through my emotions and process the grief that I'd realized that I was experiencing over the children that I would never have, the family that I would never get to care for. But now, as days had turned into weeks that would soon start to turn into months, I was grateful for the arduous work that kept my hands busy and made me collapse exhausted into bed at night.

As the floor dried, I went back up to the attic and started bringing the chairs for the dining room set downstairs. After five trips, up and down two flights of stairs, my thigh muscles were aching and turning to jelly. I placed the chairs in approximately the right position and tried to picture the room with the table and sideboard in place. It looked as if it could be a magnificent room, much grander than any room I'd ever dreamed of serving dinner in. After a quick and very late lunch, I went back upstairs for some more exploring. The attic space seemed brighter and less claustrophobic today, probably because I'd forgotten to close the window last night. I checked some of the boxes and crates by the stairs and found plates and incredibly delicate wine glasses with etched roses, so sheer that I hardly dared to touch them. I carried the boxes carefully down to the kitchen and spent most of the afternoon washing them with the utmost care, just one glass or plate in the sink at a time and drying every piece carefully instead of stacking them in the drying rack as I would have done with our regular china.

When Thomas came home, it had gone dark outside, and I'd sat for almost an hour at our small table in the breakfast nook, with dinner covered on the stove. The excitement over the fancy dining room set had shifted into frustration that I couldn't get the table downstairs by myself and had been forced to set the beautiful plates and glasses on our small and chipped IKEA table in the kitchen. It had gone dark outside, and I'd lit a couple of candles to try and brighten the dull setting, but they were halfway gone by now. The food that had smelled so very promising had congealed into a rather unsightly mess, and my good mood from before had also turned into something much less appetizing.

I'd poured myself some wine in one of the elegant glasses from the attic, and most of the contents of that glass was now sloshing around in my otherwise empty stomach. The disappointment and frustration weren't the least bit dampened by the wine, on the contrary, it made it almost worse. I was hungry—starving, in fact—but had completely lost my appetite. No piece of furniture could make up for the fact that my husband was almost an hour and a half late and hadn't bothered to call and let me know.

The loneliness that had been building over the last couple of weeks had taken on a sharp and jagged edge as I was forced to admit to myself that the one person in my life wasn't treating me very nice. What did that say about me, about our marriage, about our hope for a happy future in this giant, empty house? My thoughts ran rampant in all directions, most of them dark. I had worked my way through being worried that something might have happened to him, to annoyed that he'd not even bothered to call, to raging fury over the disrespect, that he'd let all this food go to waste and that he couldn't even be bothered to spend a couple of hours a night with me, as my sole human contact. Was I really that boring?

I was on the verge of tears when I finally heard the car pull up. I got up from the table, refilled my glass as I filled his and then tried to salvage the dinner as best I could.

The front door slammed shut behind him with such force that the whole house seemed to shake and I jumped and dropped the ladle into the pot. Then I felt my entire body tense up as I waited. It took only about half a minute or so, but I was holding my breath, and it felt like an eternity. Then Thomas sauntered into the kitchen, glaring at me with a deep frown.

"Hello," I said and forced an artificial cheerfulness into my voice in the hope of defusing his combustible mood. "How was your day?" I regretted asking that as soon as the words left my mouth. Why poke the bear that was so obviously already pissed? That was not the face of a man that had had a good day.

He grunted something, walked over to the table and more or less fell down on the chair. A couple of gulps of wine later, he turned toward me. I lifted the pot from the stove and carried it over to the table, placing it in front of him. He took one look at the contents and then pushed his empty plate away.

"I'm not sure what that's supposed to be, but I'm not eating it."

I sat down across from him, trying not to let my anger show. "It looked a lot nicer an hour and a half ago."

He grunted something again.

"You could have called ..." I started but went quiet when I saw his neck starting to go red. "You won't believe what I found in the attic," I said, with another boost of fake cheer in my voice. "A complete dining room set. I've brought the chairs down, but I need your help with the table and sideboard. They're really massive."

He collapsed back against the chair, letting out a deep sigh. "You couldn't just let me catch my breath for five minutes? I'm exhausted. The commute is killing me."

"I didn't mean *right now*," I hurried to explain, even though I had waited impatiently for hours to do this. "Whenever. Some other time." I tried to not let my disappointment show, but some of it must have been apparent, because he sighed again and then got up.

"All right, show me where it is."

I walked ahead of him up to the attic. He stopped at the top of the stairs and just stared at all the shapes in the darkness in front of him. Since I'd been up and down those stairs all day, I didn't even think about the fact that the room was in complete darkness now that it had gone dark outside.

"I can't see a damn thing," he muttered. "Isn't there a light switch somewhere?"

"I haven't been able to find one," I said. "But the table is over here."

He followed me over to it, casting glances to both sides and behind him. If I didn't know any better, I'd have thought that he was scared. "Can you grab hold of that end?" I gripped the massive wooden slab that was the top of the table and waited for him to lift the other end. He grabbed the table, and we lifted it at the same time. I could barely see his face, but he made a small noise that suggested that he hadn't been prepared for how heavy it was. I'd carried all the matching chairs, so I knew exactly what solid craftsmanship it was.

Together, we managed to get the table down both

sets of stairs, although Thomas had to put his end of the table down on several occasions and wipe his forehead. Not until we were back on the first floor did he stop throwing stolen glances in all directions. Apparently, it wasn't just me that this house was creeping out a bit. That was actually quite a relief to see.

With the table in its rightful place, I was about to go back up after the sideboard, but one look at Thomas's face made me stop. "We can get the sideboard some other time," I said. "Perhaps at the weekend."

Thomas was already on his way to the kitchen, and I followed him in there. He walked straight over to the fridge and got a beer. "I can't wait for this day to be over," he muttered and something about how grunt work was for morons without a degree. Then he disappeared out the door and up the stairs before I could say a thing.

I threw away the ruined dinner and made myself a sandwich that I washed down with another glass of wine. After I'd finished the dishes, I walked over to the dining room doorway with my beautiful wine glass in my hand, and stood there admiring my new dining room set. What a spectacular room this could be. The bare windows and walls were a bit cold and hard, but I could see the potential.

Too bad that Thomas didn't seem to care anymore.

6

As soon as Thomas had gone off to work the next morning, I headed back up to the attic. The sideboard stood where I'd left it, and I threw a longing glance at it but knew that I'd kill myself or at least break something if I tried to get the heavy piece of furniture down those stairs on my own. It would just have to wait until the weekend. Or whenever Thomas might be in the mood.

A large armoire in the corner in the back had briefly caught my attention yesterday, but since I didn't really need a wardrobe with the huge walk-in closet in the master bedroom, I had focused on the dining room furniture. This morning, at the breakfast table, I had suddenly begun to wonder if there might be something *in* it, and that was what I wanted to find out now.

The dust had settled since yesterday, and because I'd spent so much time up here now, the large space felt a lot less claustrophobic. I walked over to the imposing armoire that seemed to have intricate patterns in the front that I couldn't quite make out here in the semi-darkness. I pulled on the handle, but the doors didn't move. I stared at the cupboard, suddenly convinced that there was something in there, something that I felt anxious to discover. There was a keyhole, a large one, and I fumbled in my pocket for the other keys from the kitchen drawer. The largest one, the one I had thought would fit the attic door, slid right into the cartoonishly large keyhole and turned with a metallic groan.

I opened the wide doors with a lump of anticipation in my throat. There probably wouldn't be anything in there. Nothing worth getting so excited about, anyway. Definitely not the treasures I was getting so keyed up for.

One side of the armoire was made for hanging clothes, and the other side had shelves and a couple of drawers at the bottom. There were only a few garments hanging to the left, dresses that swayed slowly when I touched them. The fabric felt fragile under my fingers, and I didn't dare to take them out. Instead, I focused on the wide shelves to the right that were stacked high with textiles. I pulled them out and unfolded monogrammed towels, sheets, tablecloths and curtains, everything of the finest quality and well cared for up until their abandonment that must have been decades ago. It would cost a fortune to buy all this in one of those shabby chic stores in town.

When I tilted the fabrics against the light, I realized with a jolt that the curly and decorative letters that were darned into the sheets and pillowcases were my own initials. A-L-S. Anna Lisa Stevenson. I felt a chill running down my spine. What were the odds of that, of me having the same initials as some woman who had lived here before? Well, just because something was highly unlikely didn't mean that it couldn't happen. This was just a strange coincidence. Nothing more. Part of me wanted to stuff the bundles of fabric back inside the armoire, lock the doors firmly and forget all about them, but the sane part of my brain recognized the quality and beauty of the textiles and knew what difference they would make to the large, cavernous rooms downstairs.

But how was I going to hang the curtains, without curtain rods? I was certain that none of the windows in the house were built to standardized measurements and the cheap curtain rods that I might be able to afford either wouldn't fit or would just look tacky against the elegant window frames. I glanced around the attic, at all the shrouded shapes and shadows. There might very well be some here, but it could take a while before I found them. As I turned back toward the armoire, I suddenly heard a chiming sound coming from the corner furthest in, to my left. I jumped and stared into the darkness, heart pounding as I strained to make out any shapes in the corner that was almost entirely out of reach for the faint light from the windows. The clock or whatever it was chimed nine times and then the attic went quiet again. I could almost hear my own heart beating frantically against my chest and felt every muscle in my body slowly, reluctantly, start to relax as I took a couple of deep breaths and collected myself. Even though I knew that I was alone up here and that there was nothing for me to be afraid of, I could feel my skin crawl and I kept my eyes fixed on that dark corner until my vision started to blur. When I'd calmed down a little, I steeled myself, forced my legs into action and walked over toward the dark corner, moving slowly to allow my eyes to adjust to the darkness. I spotted the clock almost immediately, a beautiful floor model with brass pendulums and chains. And standing next to it, right in the corner, was a forest of tall, black rods of different lengths. Curtain rods for all the windows in the house. I let out a nervous laughter of relief and returned to my textiles.

I sorted through the deep stacks and chose the curtains I liked best and a small selection of tablecloths and bed linen, carried everything downstairs to the kitchen, set up the ironing board and got started. It took most of the morning, but the difference the fabrics made in the large, mostly empty rooms was astounding. The dining room, in particular, began to look inhabited once I'd added the curtains. There was still so much to do, but I was starting to see that it might be possible to create a home out of this cavernous empty shell. I tried not to think about the fact that I'd always considered children to be essential for a house to become a home and focused on decorating my over-sized doll house. It must have been a stunning property once. Perhaps it could be again. At least it was something to do.

When I was finished with the ironing, I brought the clock down from the attic and put it in the most obvious space, in the downstairs hallway where it would be heard all over the house. It was a beautiful piece, and not until I went to set it and wind it with the small key that I found inside the casing, did it occur to me how strange it was that it could have struck nine chimes, right on the dot, when I was upstairs in the attic this morning. The clock had stopped at 4.25 and had probably been stuck there for half a century or so.

7

I MADE a cup of tea and sat down in the breakfast nook, trying to calm my nerves. From there I could see straight into the living room and out over the ocean. I couldn't help but wonder about the people who had lived here before, and especially about the woman who shared my initials and her family. Was that the same woman whose curtains I could see moving slightly in the draught from the old windows. Had she been married? Had children? Raised a family in this house? And then what? It felt as if the previous inhabitants had taken nothing with them when they left. Like she had just walked out the door and disappeared, leaving her dresses hanging in the armoire.

Surely, the things in the attic were not the type of things that one left behind. Unless … she hadn't moved. As soon as the thought crossed my mind, I realized that it must be true and I felt a chill down my spine. Something must have happened to her. Whoever she was. Whoever she had been.

I rubbed my arms to rid myself of the goosebumps.

Perhaps I shouldn't think so much about her. It was starting to get on my nerves and the long days alone in this house would become even more unbearable if I started to believe in ghosts and jumped every time the old house shifted, or there was a creak on the stairs. It was just one of those things you had to get used to when you lived in an old house, strange noises and shadows that triggered the strangest fantasies. I needed to keep calm and not get carried away. Otherwise I might just go mad, all alone here with no one to talk to.

I finished my tea and walked back up into the attic where I gathered the rest of the curtains and tablecloths and put them back on the right shelves. Just as I was about to close the doors, I realized that I hadn't checked the two drawers underneath the shelves.

The right-hand drawer slid open easily and revealed a small stack of yellowed stationary and envelopes, a couple of small clothbound books of poetry and a fountain pen that immediately caught my eye. As I picked it up and turned it over in my hands, I noticed that there were some letters in gold on the side, and I angled it toward the closest window to see better.

Anthony Stewart.

I felt a chill running down my spine, but it was probably just a draft from the open window. A as in Anthony? But then I shook my head. No, a man wouldn't embroider his initials on bedlinen in that manner. This must be someone else. ALS's husband, perhaps? In that case, the S would stand for Stewart. A L Stewart. Married to Anthony. I put the poetry books and the fountain pen on top of the boxes by the stairs to bring them downstairs with me later.

The other drawer was not as cooperative. I pulled

the handle, banged the drawer and tried shifting it sideways a little to get it unstuck. Just as I was about to give
up, it came free, unexpectedly, and I almost fell on my
backside. The contents of the drawer spilled out on the
floor all around me. Dozens of embroidered handker-
chiefs, most of them with intricate lace. I studied the
embroidery again. A L S.

I gathered them up and folded them neatly before
trying to get the drawer back in place, but it was as
reluctant to go back in as it had been coming out. It
felt as if there was something in the way. I bent over to
see, and at the back, to one side, was something pale
that shone faintly in the darkness of the deep cavity. I
stuck my hand in and fumbled around in the dark,
feeling the hairs on the back of my neck standing
straight up when my imagination took over and
started making up things that my fingers might
encounter in there. But I found nothing furry, slimy or
with sharp teeth and claws. Instead, my fingertips
traced the contours of something hard and smooth,
and after wiggling it a little I pulled it out, trying to
shake off that eerie feeling that had gripped me. I
suddenly felt cold as ice all over my body, and the hairs
on my arms were standing straight. The wind must be
picking up outside. I studied my find. A small pale gray
book with ornate gold lettering on the front. *Diary*, it
said.

I opened the book. The owner had written their
name on the first page. Abigail Louise Stewart, it said in
a tight cursive handwriting. Abigail Louise. There she
was. I could almost picture her now, sitting at the
writing desk downstairs in my bedroom—*her* bedroom
—filling the pages of this diary with her life with her

husband. I looked over at the pen and stationary by the stairs. Anthony. Anthony and Abigail Louise.

I hurried over to the window, sat down on a crate filled with books and opened the diary to a random page.

8

———

... AND HE IS ALWAYS SO remorseful, after a fight, apologizing profusely and being so attentive, it's almost stifling. It's just that his emotions are too strong; he doesn't have the ability to control them. Not like I do. Never do I let him see something other than that which I wish him to perceive on my face or in my posture. Never do I reveal the thoughts that run through my head when he touches me. He must never know. If he did, it would be the end of me, of that I am sure.

For he is a man of strong emotions, and a man capable of great love can also harbor great hatred. And if he knew of my deceptions, I would need to fear for my safety. But there is no cause for concern. He will never know the real me. Never know the real reasons behind my wanting to marry him.

His decision to purchase this house was one of impulse, and I was certain that we would live to regret it, but I've come to appreciate our home as I've decorated it and made it my own. He doesn't care, of course, men rarely pay their furnishings any attention at all, but only yesterday, he complimented me on the paintings that I'd chosen for our dining room, the one with the lilies and the one of a lady in a garden, saying that they 'enhanced the dining experience, very nicely, indeed'. I had to bite my lip not to start crying. Fortunately, Anthony was occupied by his steak and didn't notice.

Perhaps it was a bad idea to hang those paintings, but I can't take them down now. Anthony might wonder.

9

I CLOSED the small book and stared out the open window at the waves churning endlessly against the cliffs below. So, this was who she had been, Abigail Louise Stewart. A liar. But as soon as I'd thought that, I wanted to take it back. What right did I have to judge her? Yes, it did sound as if she had been dishonest, but there might have been reasons for her behavior. Her husband sounded uncannily like my Thomas, and even though I never intentionally lied to him, a certain amount of omissions and spinning was required to keep the peace when you lived with a man with such a tempestuous temperament.

I couldn't help but feel a connection to this woman, who had lived in this very house, goodness knows how many years ago, and had struggled with her husband in much the same way I did. I wished that I could have met her—gotten to know her—so that she could have been my friend and confidante. She might have been able to relate to my problems and my unhappiness, and I to hers. I wondered if she'd had children and if she and her husband had been happy here, eventually, despite the fact that their marriage seemed to have been based on a lie of some sort.

I had no idea what type of lie it might have been and was eager to keep reading. At the same time, it felt a bit intrusive. Almost forbidden. Reading someone else's diary, it doesn't get much more taboo than that.

I walked over to the corner where I'd seen all those paintings yesterday and almost immediately found the paintings that Abigail had been writing about. They were beautiful but gave no clue as to why they would make Abigail want to cry. If they upset her so, why hang them in the dining room where she'd have to see them every day? I carried the paintings downstairs and hung them on the walls of the dining room. The hooks were still in place, and I hoped that I put the paintings on the right hook. Somehow the idea excited me, of restoring the house to exactly what it had looked like when Abigail and Anthony lived here.

She had been unhappy with her move here, just like me, but the decorating of the house had made it into a home for her and I so desperately wanted to feel like that, like I had a home, at least, if I could never have a family like the one I'd always dreamed of.

I went back up to the attic to get the diary and the rest of the things that I'd left by the stairs and carried them down to the small writing desk in the master bedroom. Everything fit neatly in place, as if they had never been removed from those drawers. Once again I felt that connection, almost a closeness. It made the hairs on my arms stand up straight, and I shivered, even though a faint sun cast late afternoon stripes over the floor next to me and the room was unusually warm. As

I sat down at the writing desk, I realized that Abigail must have sat right here, on this very spot, baring her secrets, her soul.

I took Anthony's fountain pen in my hand, unscrewed the cap and tried it, certain that it must have dried out, but the pen made a thick, black line in the margin of the diary. It looked as if it was the same pen that she'd used, or one very much like it. I put the cap back on and turned the pen over in my hand. Would she have used her husband's pen to record her secrets, the ones that she kept from him?

I raised my head and looked out over the waves, just as she must have done all those years ago. Abigail Louise. I wished that we hadn't been separated by time, that other woman and me. It felt as if we must have had so much in common. Even though I knew almost nothing about her, it still felt as if there was a bond between us, a link through time.

I leaned back, trying to picture her sitting in this very spot. Perhaps she listened for footsteps outside in the hallway as she penned her secrets, or perhaps the sound of a small child having woken up in the next room.

I picked up her diary, eager for more clues about what her life had been like, here in the space that was now occupied by me. I skimmed the pages looking for something, not sure why, but of course, it was the c-word that first caught my eye. No, not that one. The word child.

10

THE CHILD *I carry will be raised as his, and he will never know any different. He will love it and care for it as if it were his own, of that I am sure. He will be a great father; I knew that the first time I laid eyes on him, at that party at the Winchester's. I never told him, but it was the memory of him in their drawing room, looking out into that garden, where the Winchester children and their little friends played, that made me decide to marry him. The things he told me about having grown up an only child and how he was determined that he would have a whole brood one day. I couldn't relate to it at all, having been raised as one of six, but when the time came that I needed a husband, and quick, I remembered him.*

It took him long enough to understand my thinly veiled hints that he should propose, and he dallied so long with trying to gather courage that I was almost convinced that the truth would come out and I would be ruined. But he came around in time and now it will be all right. I'm sure he suspects nothing and I shall give him no reason to ever doubt the paternity of our beloved child. For it will be beloved. For me as a token of that love which I shall never again experience, and for him as a symbol of my undying devotion.

Nothing will ever come between us; of that I am certain. This is for the best; I know it to be so. I have chosen and must live with my decision.

We will be happy here, in this house. And live here, as they say, happily ever after. Oh, dear diary. I believe I felt the baby move, just as I wrote those very words. That must be a sign, surely. That I have done the right thing. I will choose to believe so, anyway, since the belief brings me great comfort.

In a while, I shall start supper. It is beginning to grow dark outside the window in front of me, and the sea is changing color. I do so love to watch that vast expanse of water. There is something so reassuring about the infallible nature of waves. They have beaten against the cliffs down below for centuries before we came here and they will continue to do so for centuries after we are gone. I find that reassuring, particularly in moments like today, when I am seized with doubts about the decisions I've made in my life.

In a hundred years or more, it will not make any difference at all, no matter how I fret. Not to me, not to Anthony. Perhaps to this small miracle, fluttering beneath the fabric of my dress. Perhaps this little creature, as of yet unborn, will be a wise old soul by then, surrounded by children and grandchildren in this very house.

I like that image. I wasn't entirely convinced of Anthony's decision to move out here, far away from everything and everyone, but when I think of all the children that will grow up here and their children after them ... It is a family home, truly. Perhaps they will tell stories of us, of great grandmother Abigail and great grandfather Anthony. Of how we met and fell in love and came to live here in the house by the sea.

The stories will, of course, be false and untrue, like our love. The truth makes for such poor stories, don't you think, dear Diary? The truth is best kept here, on your very pages. I am so very grateful that I have you to confide in so that I am never compelled to tell a living soul the truth. It is so much easier to lie all the time if I can confide in you the honest truth.

Oh, dear Diary. I have so much to tell you. But no more today. It is almost dark, and I fear Anthony will be back before dinner is finished.

11

I STARED out the window at the gray and turbulent sea below. Abigail's "infallible" waves. The deception and treachery on the pages before me had left a faint and unpleasant taste in my mouth, and my perception of the woman who had lived here before me had started to shift. I felt almost dizzy, having read the faded, cursive words in an unfamiliar handwriting that in parts felt so very alien to me. I couldn't imagine ever lying to Thomas about something as significant as the paternity of a child. That was like lying to one's entire family—to history, even. Abigail had perhaps been a slightly different woman than the one I had first imagined her to be.

And yet, other parts of this diary still felt as if I could have written them myself. Well, not the part about feeling a flutter underneath her dress. I would never know what that felt like, not now. But the rest. Of being trapped in marriage to a man with strong emotions, both of love and of anger. Of never feeling completely able to be oneself and speak one's mind or even tell the truth, out of fear of the consequences. Those parts of her story I could certainly relate to.

I wanted so desperately to keep reading, to perhaps find out what had happened to them, to Abigail and Anthony and the child that was still just a flutter under Abigail's dress here in the pages that I had read. Perhaps it had all worked out for the best. Perhaps Anthony had been a loving father. Perhaps Abigail had eventually fallen in love with the man she had chosen to spend her life with? Perhaps they had lived happily ever after here in this house, having many more children and grand-children. Grown old together.

But I knew deep in my heart that they couldn't have. I could feel the faint scent of a tragedy waiting to happen on the pages I had just read. And I was eager to keep reading, to follow Abigail through the pages until the diary ended. But I just couldn't stomach it. Not if it was going to end badly. If it did, I didn't want to know about it.

Instead, I tucked the diary away in one of the drawers of the writing desk and went downstairs to get the bed linen that I'd ironed earlier and hung out on the washing line to air out. I made up the bed completely with the vintage sheets that now smelled of nothing but salt and sea, and then hung the curtains that I'd chosen for our bedroom. Since the wallpaper was such a tricky color to match, I'd resigned myself to a set of neutral beige curtains, but even though they had looked pretty bland in our bright kitchen, the softness of the light fabric immediately made the slightly darker bedroom feel warmer and much more welcoming. As I stood in the doorway, I realized that this was most likely the room that Abigail and Anthony had shared, and that this might be pretty much exactly as it had looked like when they lived here, apart from the TV. It felt both comforting and disturbing at the same time.

As I was leaving the bedroom, I glanced over my shoulder one last time, and just as I turned, a dark cloud blocked out the pale autumn sun. In a second, the room went from gloomy to cloaked in semi-darkness. It was just my imagination, playing tricks on me, in the rational part of my mind I knew that, but the hairs on the back of my neck stood straight up, and I could have sworn that there was a woman standing over by the desk, opening the drawer to the left; the same one that I'd been looking in when the window up in the attic slammed shut.

12

I BLINKED and she was gone, but the vague image of her was imprinted on my retina. She'd had dark hair, just like me, about the same height and ordinarily probably the same weight, but even though her back had been slightly toward me as she'd bent over the writing desk, I could have sworn that her shape seemed heavy with pregnancy. Her clothes had been vintage-y and unfashionable but elegant and expensive looking. I stared at the desk, but the woman was nowhere to be seen now.

I shook my head. That was weird. I probably shouldn't have been thinking so much about Abigail and Anthony. My imagination was apparently starting to run wild, out here in the loneliness. I so desperately needed someone to talk to, that much was obvious. I glanced over at the desk again—no, there was no one there, of course there wasn't—and then went back up to the attic to continue my exploring.

There were several crates of books over by the window, and I brought them down, one armful at the time, and put them in the built-in bookshelves in the otherwise still empty front room. It looked a bit weird, with all those books and not a stick of furniture, but they added a little color and made the room look slightly less desolate.

It took several hours to empty just three crates, but as I opened the fourth, I gasped out loud. On top of what looked like a complete set of severely outdated encyclopedias lay a large, leather-bound photo album. I immediately forgot all about the books, put the lid back on the crate and hurried down to the bedroom, where I threw myself on the bed and opened the album to the first page.

The pages were large and square and covered with thin white paper to protect the photos from sticking to one another. I gently lifted the flimsy silk paper and looked at the first page. There was just one photo, mounted at the center of the page. A wedding photo. The names and date were printed neatly by hand underneath, with added swirls for decoration. It was them! Anthony and Abigail. I felt my heart pounding as I studied the small, faded photo for details.

The man was in a morning coat, with a funny, stiff little collar and a wide tie. His striped trousers and black-and-white shoes looked almost too frivolous in contrast to his severe facial expression, staring straight at the camera. The sun was behind him, and most of his face was in shadow, but I thought that I could make out straight, handsome features and a piercing stare underneath thick dark eyebrows. His back was almost unnaturally straight, and the shoulders were pulled back, as if he was standing to attention. One of his hands was resting on the back of a chair where a woman was sitting. She was turned a little to the side, and the setting sun made the contours of her pretty little face almost light up. Her cheeks were round and the nose small and perky, and the lips were curled in a mischievous smile. I'd never seen a more mismatched couple. Her frilly white wedding dress in contrast with his black morning suit. Her smile to his frown. Her voluptuous curves to his slim, straight figure. If the photo hadn't been so old, I would have guessed that it had been photoshopped together from two different wedding photos. I could understand what he had seen in her; everything about her signaled that this was a woman that made men lose their heads. But what had she seen in him?

Sure, he was handsome enough, judging by what little of his face I could see. But he didn't look very cheerful and didn't look the least bit in love, even though this was his wedding day. I looked a bit closer, but couldn't see anything that would suggest that this woman was in for a treat later that night. He looked like the type of man that would just want to get it over with to produce an heir and then never bother again. My eyes wandered over to the woman again. She, on the other side …

Perhaps she had managed to warm him up, make him loosen up and enjoy life a little. A wife like that ought to wipe the frown of a man's face. But then I remembered her diary and looked at them both again, from a slightly different perspective.

If this photo was taken on their wedding day, then Abigail was already pregnant, carrying another man's child as she walked down the aisle toward her future husband. Anthony didn't look like the type of man that would marry a woman to save her reputation. He didn't look like the forgiving type either.

So, what had happened to them? Had they managed to overcome the lies that their marriage was founded on? Had they lived happily ever after in this monstrosity of a house? I glanced at the ceiling and thought about all the things up there. All their things. No, it didn't look as if Abigail had gotten her happily ever after.

I turned the pages of the photo album, looking closely at every photo. There weren't many, and most of them seemed to be from the wedding. Several photos of people in their wedding attire posing stiffly in front of the photographer. Abigail with an older couple that were probably her parents. Anthony with an old, frail-looking woman that was probably his mother. Random strangers smiling politely at the camera. The dresses were lovely, even though it was hard to make out any details in the old, poor quality photos. The men looked silly and stiff in their formal attire.

The last pages displayed a handful of smaller photos taken with a different camera. Anthony and Abigail in front of the Eiffel Tower. Sacré-Cœur. Notre Dame. They must have honeymooned in Paris. But in none of the pictures did it seem like Abigail had managed to soften up her rather stiff husband. He was as straight-backed in the last photo of them as he'd been in the wedding photo. Too bad, because judging by the better lit photos from Paris, he'd been a good-looking man, with a piercing stare that usually indicated that there was a lot going on inside that handsome head. He was tall and slim and the arm that was usually wrapped protectively around his pretty little wife looked muscular and toned under the constantly buttoned-up shirts.

Abigail smiled the same sweet smile in almost all the photos, except for a couple of the last ones in Paris where she looked almost sad and wistful. Had it become apparent that this marriage wouldn't be everything that she'd hoped for? Already on the honeymoon? That was sad.

On the very last page was a single photo of a grand old house and it took a while before I realized that it was this house, my house. Abigail was standing alone on the porch, which was covered in flower boxes and planters. The whole house looked freshly painted, and all the windows were curtained with flowers or lamps in them. She looked pretty much the same as in all the other photos, so it must have been taken as they arrived back from their honeymoon. Perhaps it was the day she moved in, even.

I looked closely, but couldn't see any sign of her pregnancy showing, not even when I knew her truth. Had she managed to keep her secret? If she wasn't showing, then she mustn't have gotten pregnant long before the wedding. Could she pass off her baby as being born prematurely? A few weeks, perhaps even a month, but not much more than that, surely?

I stared at the woman on the porch, trying to picture what she must have felt like, standing there, outside her grand new house, a newlywed with a baby on the way. Had she been afraid of her husband discovering her secret? Had she been nauseated by morning sickness?

Had she turned after this photo was taken and walked in that front door, happy to start her new life or dreading it? Had Anthony carried her over the threshold? He didn't look the type for romantic gestures.

But then, you never knew. He was a man of strong emotions. Perhaps he'd turned out to be passionate in bed as well? I smiled a little and turned the pages back to look at the photos of him again. None of them showed what he looked like smiling, and I found myself thinking that it was a shame. Such a handsome man. I hoped that Abigail had made him happy.

I lay back on the pillows, looking up at the ceiling. Had they laid together here, Abigail and her husband, right in the spot where Thomas and I slept? It was the only place in the room where a double bed would fit, so if this had been their bedroom, they must have. I closed my eyes and tried to picture them here, on their first night back from Paris. Abigail coming in the door, dressed in something white and frilly and perhaps even a little sexy. If she'd already been pregnant at the wedding, she'd have needed him to make love to her often, to make it likely that she'd conceived already on their honeymoon. Had she kept it up when they'd returned? Had she seduced him right here where I was laying? I tried to picture the man from the photos climbing on top of his wife and kissing her passionately, but I just couldn't. He didn't seem like the type. Too stiff, and not in a good way.

But he had been handsome, though. I smiled and rolled over on my side, trying to picture him on the pillow next to me, where Thomas used to lay. My husband was also handsome, but not as intensely so as Anthony had been. And he was dark, like Anthony had been. Abigail and I apparently had the same taste in men.

Too bad that's where the similarities ended, I thought, and rolled over on my back, placing one hand on my flat stomach.

THAT EVENING I prepared a nice dinner and set the table in the dining room with the pretty china and the lovely rose-etched glasses. Our first dinner in our grand dining room. It felt like an occasion worthy of a celebration. I put on some makeup and a dress and found some soft music on my phone that I played via Thomas's Bluetooth speaker that I'd hidden behind the new curtains. The paintings looked spectacular and I was almost giddy with excitement when I stirred the sauce and listened for Thomas's car.

He'd promised that he'd be home by 7, 7.30 at the latest, but when the clock in the hallway chimed 8, there was still no sign of him. I poured myself a glass of wine and walked into the hallway, staring out into the darkness. The extent of my isolation suddenly struck me. What would I do if he didn't come home one day? What would I do if something happened to him?

I felt the panic start to build and took a big gulp of wine to try and calm my nerves. Nothing was going to happen to him. And of course he would always come home at the end of the day. He must have just been delayed for some reason. Things happened.

At 8.20, I finally spotted his headlights coming up the road through the trees. My wine glass was empty and the taste of the wine had turned sour on my tongue, but I shook off the worry and went back out into the kitchen to check on the food. I'd learned my lesson and chosen something that would keep this time. I carried the food into the dining room and poured wine for us both. I heard the front door open and close—not slam shut this time—and breathed a sigh of relief. The evening was salvaged. This could still be a nice meal.

I heard him walk into the kitchen and call my name.

"In here!" I called back.

I turned toward the door, waiting expectantly to see the look on his face as he saw the finished room. He appeared in the doorway, loosening his tie.

"What are you doing in here?" He regarded the table suspiciously. "Did I forget our anniversary or something?"

I laughed to try and cover up my disappointment. "No, of course not."

"Is it your birthday, then? Or mine?" He pulled off his tie and leaned against the doorframe.

"No," I said, indicating his chair with my hand. "Please, take a seat. Dinner is ready."

"I've already eaten," he said, shoving his tie into his pocket. "I'm knackered, so I'm just going to go to bed. I've got an early meeting in the morning ..."

Before I could protest or even just say anything, he was gone. "B-but ..." I stuttered, but the doorway was empty and I could hear heavy footsteps up the stairs. I turned and looked at the beautifully set table, the lit candles, the curtains, the paintings. Then I looked down at my dress, the pretty shoes and the floor that I had scrubbed on my hands and knees.

What just happened? I walked slowly over to the table, sitting down. The tears in my eyes made the candles blurry, and I started to reach for the wine bottle but stopped myself. No, Lisa. No more.

I felt sick. Sick with loneliness, sick with grief over my life that I'd never get to live, sick with anger over the way my husband was treating me. Was I overreacting? Perhaps a little. But I didn't think that it was too much to ask, that a husband spent half an hour or so at the dinner table with his wife that he hadn't seen all day. I had things I wanted to tell him. I wanted to know about his day.

But the truth that was slowly starting to dawn on me was that Thomas couldn't care less about mine.

I blew out the candles and put the food away in the fridge. When I came up to the bedroom, the lights were out, and Thomas seemed to be sleeping. I went into the bathroom to wash off my makeup and brush my teeth. When I dropped my clothes in the hamper, I noticed Thomas's shirt hanging over the edge. I pulled on the sleeve to drop it all the way in, but just as I was about to let go, I noticed a stain on the collar. It looked almost like blood. I sighed and pulled the shirt all the way out of the hamper. If I was going to get that stain out, I'd need to soak the shirt in cold water immediately. But when I held the shirt up closer to the faint light above the mirror, I realized that it wasn't blood.

It was lipstick.

I WALKED back downstairs and through the dark and empty rooms with tears running down my face. It was late and I was exhausted but I couldn't stand the thought of going to bed next to my husband who apparently had spent the evening with another woman. There might be a perfectly reasonable explanation, a small part of my brain was saying, but the rest of me wouldn't listen. There was only one explanation and that was that my life that had seemed to be pretty ruined already had taken a sharp turn for the worse. Oh, Thomas, how could you? First, he'd crushed my dreams when he'd spent all my money on this horrible house and now ...

It had all been for nothing. No matter what I did or how hard I worked, we would never be happy here. Thomas didn't even want to live here. He hadn't bought the house for us, as a home for us two. It had just been an investment to him, but his big plans had fallen through and now the house reminded him of his failure, of all the money he'd thought he'd make on a quick flip, that he'd planned to use for goodness knows what.

He'd been so frustrated by the contractors who'd all thought that he was an idiot to have bought this old monstrosity, and now we were stuck here. It was typical of him, he often ran hot and cold like that, especially when things didn't go as planned. Now he was angry and disappointed, frustrated and burying himself in work to avoid facing the reality of what he'd done. But the work didn't seem to take his mind of the situation and he was always complaining about the commute. And now he'd found someone else, back in town. What was he planning to do? Just leave me here?

The loneliness that I'd been walking around in like a fog closed in on me, and it felt as if I couldn't breathe, even though I was surrounded by nothing but empty spaces. This was not the way it was supposed to be. I'd been working hard to make this monstrosity into a home for us, and we were going to be happy here ... no, not happy, perhaps ... but I was going to make the effort, and together we were going to make the best of a difficult situation, just like Anthony and Abigail had. As soon as I'd thought that, I was filled with dread. What if we were just like them, cursed from the start? What if that was the reason that we'd never had children, because we just weren't meant to be? Because no matter what I did, we were never going to be happy?

I buried my face in my hands but suddenly realized that I could hear music playing softly somewhere nearby. Oh, Thomas's speaker. I'd left my cell phone playing in the dining room. I dried my tears and walked over to the double sliding doors, pulling them aside gently. When I'd closed them earlier, so that we wouldn't need to see the empty living room, the doors had creaked shut on rusty rails, but now they moved apart without so much as a squeak.

I slapped my hand in front of my mouth to keep the gasp that escaped me from being heard. The room was not empty. The candles that I'd blown out were lit again, and the table was set, not just with the two place settings and the serving bowls that I'd put out when Thomas came home, but with carafes and flowers as well, and I was not alone down here, as I'd supposed. A man and a woman were sitting across from each other, and the man was raising his glass, his wine glass with etched roses, toward the woman and toasted her as he nodded appreciatively toward the paintings on the wall. The woman raised her own glass in reply, and when the man put his glass down and turned his attention toward the piece of meat on his plate, she took her napkin and dabbed discretely at her eyes.

I bit my lip to keep from screaming, and suddenly they were gone. The room was dark and quiet, the table was empty, and the music that I'd heard had gone silent. I clung to the doors, waiting for my pounding heart to return to its regular pace, blinking frantically to rid myself of the image I'd seen. It was just my imagination, I knew that, but it had seemed so very real. That stupid diary, I should never have read it. Well, there's your punishment for snooping through other people's things, I thought, and forced myself to walk through the dark room toward the window sill. My phone and the speaker was behind the curtain where I'd left them, and there was a small light coming from the speaker, an indication that I'd forgotten to switch it off, but when I picked up my phone the display didn't light up, and when I pressed the button, the battery icon flashed briefly and then the screen went black again.

It must have just gone out. I must have left it on when I went upstairs, and it had kept playing, and the music must have made me imagine that I saw the scene that I'd read about in the diary, and when the battery ran out, I came to my senses again. Yes, that must have been what happened.

It was just my imagination. I was not starting to go mad.

At least, I hoped not.

15

Eventually, I went upstairs and crawled into bed, as far away from my husband as possible, curled up into a little ball, right on the edge of the mattress. Despite the fatigue that made my entire body ache, it took a while before I fell asleep and I was forced to lay there, listening to Thomas's heavy breathing. Nothing seemed to disturb his beauty sleep. Whatever had happened, he didn't feel guilty about it.

After a while I must have fallen asleep because I woke up with a start and a throbbing headache when I heard the front door slam shut downstairs. I sat up straight. The room was lit by a faint streak of light that slipped in between the curtains. Thomas. No. He couldn't just leave. We had to talk about this. We had to …

I scrambled out of bed and out onto the landing, almost breaking my neck as I hurried down the steep stairs and over to the front door. I threw it open and ran over the wet porch on bare feet, yelling at the top of my voice.

"Thomas! Wait! Stop!"

But he didn't hear me. The car was almost out of sight, and before I could catch my breath to yell again, it was gone. I shuddered and wrapped my arms around me. It was cold outside, really cold, and I hurried back inside.

The house seemed even lonelier than before, and the soft chimes from the clock as it struck seven kept echoing in my ears as I returned upstairs. I had so many things on my To-do-list, but as I stared at the bed with the rumpled sheets, I just couldn't muster up the energy to do anything at all. What was the point? Why should I work so hard to build a home for us, when he didn't care? Not about the house and obviously not about me.

I crawled back under the covers and tried to get back to sleep, but I just tossed and turned and eventually I got up and went downstairs. I made some coffee and a sandwich and curled up in the breakfast nook. The doors to the dining room were closed, but when I closed my eyes, I could hear the music coming from inside and hear the clinking of china and crystal glasses.

It had seemed so very real. Almost more real than my own life. And as I remembered it now, I was amazed at the level of detail that my imagination had managed to come up with. I could remember the shape and color of the man's cufflinks and the gentle way the woman had dabbed at her eyes as they teared up. She'd had a large wedding ring on her hand, and a brooch on the front of her dress and there had been a napkin ring on the tablecloth beside her plate and …

Where had I got all that from? There had been no mention of jewelry or napkin rings or flower arrangements in Abigail's diary. And I'd never had such vivid daydreams before, not so that I'd been uncertain as to whether what I'd seen had been real or not.

I rubbed my forehead and stared at the wall. What on earth was I going to do? I tried to think of some way out of this hopeless situation, but my temples throbbed and the coffee tasted like mud. The lack of sleep and the disappointment I felt when I remembered the stain on my husband's collar made me just want to give up.

I poured the coffee down the sink and walked into the hallway. It was early, still, and my plan had originally been to get started on one of the rooms upstairs that might eventually be made into a guest room. But who was I trying to fool? There wouldn't be any guests. There was no point in starting to tear down the old wallpaper or scrub any more floors. Thomas wouldn't thank me. In fact, he wouldn't even care.

Instead of getting the bucket from the utility room, I went into the front room and picked out a novel from the built-in shelves. I brought it upstairs to the bedroom, crawled under the covers and started to read.

I AWOKE WITH A START, sat up and looked around me. The light outside had started to change, and there was a chill in the air. I must have fallen asleep, and been awoken by a sound that could no longer be heard. There it was again. A knock on the door. I closed the book that lay on the covers next to me, and hurried out of bed.

The house was dark, and I switched on the lights as I went. How long had I been asleep? What time was it? It felt late. I hurried to the front door and opened it. Outside stood a little old lady with a cake tin in her hands and a tall man with golden curls tumbling down his forehead. I stared at them.

"Er … Hi?"

"Hello, dear." The old woman stepped forward, thrusting the cake tin at my midriff. "I'm Holly Kensington, from next door!" She pointed over her shoulder at the house down the hill. "Your neighbor!" she added as if I hadn't been able to draw that conclusion already.

"Oh, nice to meet you," I said and reached out my hand to greet the woman. "I'm Lisa. Lisa Stevenson."

The woman placed the cake tin in my outreached hand. "Nice to meet you, Lisa. And this here is my son, Freddy. He's visiting, and I made him drive me up here. If I waited until my George got around to it, we would never have met. How long have you lived here now? A month?"

I shook my head slowly. "Only about a couple of weeks," I said. "We moved in on the first of this month."

"That recently? It felt like longer. Well, time flies, eh?" The woman took a step back. "I just wanted to say hello and let you know that if you should ever need anything, me and George are just down the hill."

"That's very kind," I said and stepped to the side. "Would you like to come in?"

The small woman's smile disappeared and was replaced with a wide-eyed stare. "Oh, no. No offense, but I'm not setting foot inside that house. Not ever."

Her son shook his head and muttered something that sounded like "Mother!" under his breath.

I reached past the old woman and shook his hand. "Well, it was nice meeting you both," I said and held up the cake tin. "And thank you so much for this, whatever it is."

"Just some lemon bars, dear. A little housewarming gift. I thought you could use some … warming."

"Mother," said the tall man again, this time loud enough that everyone heard him. "I'm sorry," he said to me. "My mother has gotten it into her head that this house is haunted." He smiled apologetically. "It's so embarrassing. Don't mind her. It's just superstition. She's been reading too many trashy novels."

Mrs. Kensington harrumphed. "Too many novels? There's no such thing! You mind how you speak to me, young man. You're not too old for me to put you over my knee …"

I couldn't help but smile. The man was quite obviously too old to be put over anyone's knee. He was tall and muscular and would have been rather intimidating if it hadn't been for those blond angelic curls that bounced when he moved and the dimples that appeared on both sides of his wide smile. I felt myself go warm inside and immediately took a small step back, grabbing the door for … safety? Not that the man felt like any kind of threat, but the emotions that he stirred inside of me felt lethal.

"Well, we must be going," he said. "I've got to be in town in an hour to pick up my kids."

The warmth inside of me went out like a candle in a crosswind. "Oh, you have kids?" I mumbled.

"Three," he said, and the smile glowed with even more intensity. This time it didn't create a responding glow inside of me, though. It just shone a light on the void in my heart where my own children should have taken up space. "And if I'm not exactly on time, my ex is going to tell them all sorts of terrible things about me, so I'd better be going."

"Oh," I said, unsure what to do with all that information. Three children and an ex-wife. How had he had time for all that? He must be at least five years younger than me. I heard a car coming up the driveway and looked up to see Thomas coming home from work. Oh, right. This guy hadn't married the wrong person and spent a decade trying to make things right. That would give a person plenty of time for other things.

Thomas parked his car as I said goodbye and when the neighbor woman and her son walked back to their car, they met him and shook hands briefly. I didn't hear what they said but remained in the doorway watching the interaction. I couldn't help comparing the two men, standing side by side. Darkness and light, I thought, and immediately felt guilty. Then I shook my head to rid myself of that feeling. I hadn't done anything to feel guilty about.

And then the memories from last night came crashing down on me, and I almost fell to my knees with sadness as I remembered the lipstick and all the ways I had imagined that it might have ended up on my husband's shirt. Oh, Thomas. How could you? The sadness hit me like a wet towel in the face, and I shivered where I stood on the doorstep. I had never felt so alone in my life, so cold, so empty. The blond man helping his mother into his car out there in the driveway exuded warmth, I could feel it all the way from here, and it took all my energy not to run to him and beg him to take me with him. That was the kind of man I should have married. The kind of man who could have given me the life I'd always dreamed of. Lots of kids and a close-knit family. Not Thomas, who had crushed my dreams and my spirit and then stuck me here in this remote house, where I would slowly go mad while he was off doing who knows what with god knows who.

I was gripped by hatred toward my husband, unlike anything I had ever felt before. For the first time, I allowed myself to acknowledge the truth about my marriage. We weren't in love anymore, hadn't been for years. He had stolen the money I'd planned to use for

IVF, and now he'd probably cheated on me, as well. It was his fault that I'd never have any children. His fault that I'd never be happy. This marriage was dead. Just like I felt, inside.

When the neighbors drove off, Thomas waved at them and then walked up the stairs toward me. I had to struggle not to let my newly freed emotions show on my face.

"So, this is what you do when I'm not around?" he said, and the hatred in his voice was obvious to me, since I had just felt something similar myself. "Entertain strange men?"

I just stared at him. "Mrs. Kensington from next door? She stopped by with some lemon bars. A house warming gift. God knows we needed that."

I pushed the cake tin into his hands and stalked back inside the house, confused and confounded by all the emotions welling up inside of me. I wanted nothing more than to get out of here, get out of this marriage and leave this miserable existence, but there was nowhere for me to go, no one that I could turn to.

I was all alone, and the only person in my life didn't care the least bit about me.

I MADE it almost all the way up the stairs before Thomas caught up with me. His firm grip made me lose my footing on the worn and slippery steps, and I fell, hard, just barely managing to brace myself.

"Don't you dare speak to me that way," he growled and turned me over to face him. "I work so hard all day for us, and I don't do it so that you can spend all this time screwing other men behind my back!"

I just stared at him. As ridiculous as his accusations were, coming from a man who'd just last night come home with lipstick on his collar, I couldn't help but remember the longing inside of me for that man who had just been here with his mother. If he had wanted to sleep with me, I would have gladly obliged. If only. He looked as if he would make the experience a completely pleasurable one, for both of us. I shook my head. And this was my husband, standing over me on the hard stairs, looking as if he wanted to kill me. Perhaps I should let him? Perhaps I should even encourage him?

"Well, someone has to do it," I spat at him. "You're not around."

He stared at me, and I wasn't sure if it was the words that were unexpected coming from me or if it was the unusually sharp tone of my voice. "Get up!" he hissed and grabbed me hard by the arm. He pulled me up and dragged me up the rest of the stairs and into the bedroom. There, he threw me on the bed and stood next to the bed panting, staring down at me.

I sat up, rubbing my arm where I could still feel the steel grip of his fingers, and shook my head. "Honestly," I said and tried to keep the anger I felt out of my voice. It worked like catnip on him, triggering his own rage. "That man is our neighbor's son. He drove his mother here so that she could drop of a housewarming gift. I just met him, ten minutes ago. He is right now on his way back to his family in the city. His three children! Where in this image do you manage to fit in a torrid affair?" I stood up and took a cautious step closer to my husband. "Don't you think that you might have been a bit hasty with your accusations?" I said, quietly debating whether I should say something about the lipstick on his shirt.

Thomas shook me off. "Accusations?" he said. "Well, if the shoe fits …"

I shook my head. "But it doesn't. It really doesn't. I haven't met a soul since we moved here, apart from Mrs. Kensington and her son, just now."

He stared at me. "I saw the way you looked at him," he said, and it took all my efforts not to cringe as I remembered the powerful emotions that the stranger had awoken inside of me.

"I didn't …" I said and moved away. "I wouldn't. But

if that is how you feel …" I could see myself, as if from above, an out-of-body experience, watching myself taking a step I didn't really dare to. "Perhaps that is a sign. Perhaps we should call it quits. Perhaps we should start discussing a divorce."

He scoffed at me and took a step closer, crowding me up against the edge of the bed. "Divorce?" He raised his hand, and as it moved closer to my face, I had to force myself to not back away. His caress felt like a slap. I would have preferred it if he had hit me. It would have been less painful. "What on earth are you talking about? We're not getting a divorce. I would never leave you, sweetheart, not ever," he said, moving closer so that I could feel his warm breath against my ear. "And you are never, ever, leaving me. You are my wife," he whispered and kissed me gently on the cheek. "Until death do us part, remember."

I went cold. There was no doubt in my mind that he meant it. That regardless of how empty and meaningless our marriage became, regardless of how many shades of lipstick was on his collar when he came home late at night, he would never admit that our marriage had been a mistake. This was it. For the rest of our lives. This was my future. Until death … "I'm starving," I said, pulling away. "You must be too. I'm starting dinner."

I hurried downstairs, praying that he wouldn't follow me until he'd had time to calm down.

Was this what it had been like for Abigail? Had she also been hiding from her husband in their own home? Had she lived a lie, only brief stolen moments of truth alone with her diary, that she must have kept hidden away somewhere in the house? Had she feared what would happen if her husband, Anthony, found it?

Had he found it?

My hands trembled as I got the ingredients for dinner from the refrigerator.

Was that what had happened? Had Anthony been just like Thomas, refusing to accept that things hadn't turned out the way he had planned when they had said their vows all those years ago? And Abigail's and Anthony's marriage had been founded on a lie, even more fragile from the start than mine and Thomas's.

How had Anthony reacted when he found out? What had happened to them?

And what was going to happen to me?

Something had changed between us, and I felt something changing inside of me as well over the next couple of days. I started working on the house again, cleaning, fixing, getting things in order. For what, I wasn't sure. I no longer planned for a future in this house. I wasn't sure that I had a future to plan for, at all. If this was what it was going to be like, forever, then what was the point? The hard work kept me busy, but it didn't occupy my mind. The only upside was that I collapsed from exhaustion every night and didn't have to lie sleepless alongside a man who no longer reached for me.

That part of our marriage was the only thing we'd had after the first exhilaration of falling in love had faded, and now we didn't even have that. I didn't miss it, my body was too worn out after all the cleaning and restoring to even want to spend the effort of making up with Thomas, but I felt the loneliness more intensely than ever.

Instead, I moved from room to room in the large

house, checking item after item off the never-ending list of chores and tasks. My whole body ached after hours of scrubbing, sanding, carrying heavy furniture from room to room and down the stairs from the attic. And most of the time I was alone. Thomas's long days at work got even longer, and I didn't mind. He started eating dinner in the city, before the long drive out to the house, and I didn't bother cooking just for me. Sandwiches and tea, looking out over the sea that never seemed to change color from that depressing gray.

One afternoon, I came downstairs after spending most of the day pulling the peeling wallpaper off the walls in one of the many rooms that I had no idea what we were going to do with. How many guest rooms could a couple have, if they never even intended to have any guests? I sighed and shook my head. What was the point? Why was I doing this? For whom? Looking around the living room, still relatively bare, without the sofas that I could picture over by the fireplace, I felt no pleasure in all the hard work I had put in and all the changes and improvements I had made. Yes, the room looked a lot nicer now. But no one was ever going to see it. The only person who had even come to the house, that quirky little neighbor lady, would never even dare to set foot inside of it. I couldn't help but smile. As dreary and dark and abandoned as this house might seem, I hadn't seen any traces of any ghosts. Nothing out of the ordinary, apart from the brief figments of my own imagination, and they had stopped when I put the diary away.

I hadn't even felt the presence of Abigail again, even though I slept in her bedroom—between her monogrammed sheets—ate at her dinner table and drank from her wine glasses. That woman I had felt such a connection with when we first moved in was long gone and no amount of imagining would change that. In a weird way I almost missed her, and I instantly regretted that I hadn't read more of her diary. It was the closest that I'd been to another human being for weeks. Pitiful, really.

Suddenly I felt the fatigue of all that hard work and decided to let the rest of the wallpaper wait until another day. Thomas wouldn't care. He never asked me what I'd done when he came home in the evenings, or even noticed it, even if I had made changes to the few rooms that he frequented. Why we should live in this awful house when he didn't even care about it was beyond me. I wished I was back in town, in our small and cramped apartment. I hadn't had any family or friends there either, but I'd at least had my co-workers for a few hours most weekdays and I was just now starting to realize how much our mundane small talk had meant to me. Without even some basic human interaction I would start to go mad, but there was no one here I could turn to, no one to talk to, to vent to about Thomas and what he might be doing behind my back.

I desperately needed a friend, someone to confide in, but as I didn't have that, I decided to settle for the one human connection I had felt since I'd moved to this horrible house. It was at least better than nothing. Not by much, that was true, but I was in no position to be picky.

I walked back upstairs to my bedroom and retrieved

Abigail's diary from the drawer in the writing desk. Curling up on the bedspread, wrapping a blanket around my legs, I opened the book to a random page and started reading.

19

Dear Diary, if he found out ... I can't bear to think of what that might entail. Then it would all be over. Our marriage, for sure, and perhaps even my life.

Our lives. I can't help placing my hand on my belly as I am writing this. Because it is so very obvious to me now that this is not about me anymore. There is another being, right here inside of me, that is still so very dependent on me for its life. I don't care what happens to me, but this little life, the only good thing that ever came from me, this I must protect at all cost.

The thing I fear most is that the child itself will be proof of my infidelity. Both Anthony and I have dark hair and brown eyes. What if my child has blond curls and blue eyes? They say all infants have blue eyes, and that it changes with time, so perhaps I can get away with it for a few weeks. Months, perhaps? I don't know. I pray and pray that the child will have inherited its mother's dark curls and olive complexion. Let it be like its father in character and temperament only. An artist of immense talent, a gentle and kind soul, unlike my dull husband who grows more severe with every day that passes.

I don't know how he could have found out, but there has been a change in his behavior toward me over the last couple of weeks. As much as I hate to admit it, he might have uncovered some things about my past that I'd rather he didn't know about. I can't think who might have told him, but have resolved that he'll never learn the truth from me. I've had a writing desk made for the bedroom, a pretty little thing with a secret compartment, the perfect hiding place for my treasures ...

20

I GLANCED over at the writing desk. A secret compartment? I got up and hurried over to it. I had checked it
quite thoroughly before bringing it down from the attic,
and I'd gone over it with a damp rag to clean out what
little dust had snuck in under the dust cloth, but hadn't
noticed anything out of the ordinary. I ran my fingers
over the top, the back and both sides, and then sat down
and felt around underneath the small desk. Nothing. No
knobs or levers, no sections that came off, even if I
pushed them or tried to slide them.

I hurried back to the bed and checked the rest of the
page, but Abigail hadn't written anything more about
the desk or the secret compartment. When I went to put
the diary back in the left bottom drawer, I suddenly
remembered the odd feeling I'd had up in the attic the
first time I found it, and the vision I'd had of the woman
standing by the desk. Sure, it was just stupid fantasies,
but in both cases, it had been this drawer. I sat down on
the chair and pulled the drawer all the way toward me,

completely out of its slot. It was a deep and rather narrow space and I couldn't see the back of it, so I hurried over to my nightstand and got the flashlight. When I directed it at the hollow square, something glinted in the back. Something small and fairly roundish. A keyhole!

I threw the flashlight on the bed and ran out into the hall and into the bathroom, where I pulled my jeans out of the hamper. I'd been carrying the last of the keys from the kitchen drawer around with me for weeks and not found a keyhole that matched. Could it be …?

My heart was pounding in my chest and I wasn't sure why. It was probably just some love letters from the man who was the real father of her child. I already knew of her infidelity so why did I get so excited? But when the key fit perfectly and turned without so much as a squeak, I laughed out loud. I heard a clicking sound somewhere to the side and when I leaned over, I could see that the bottom part of the side of the desk had opened up. I pulled at it, and a whole section of the desk slid out, like a flat drawer that ran along the entire bottom of the desk. The compartment stuck about halfway out, but it was more than enough to see what was in it.

A small bundle of love letters, tied with a lilac ribbon, addressed to Miss Abigail Thornton at an address in a small town that I thought was a bit further up north along the coast. Some jewelry and small mementos, a couple of smooth stones, a feather with an interesting pattern, a book of matches from a hotel in some place called Riva del Garda and some faded photos. At first, I couldn't make out what was on them, but then my eyes made sense of the shapes and I realized that I was looking at two naked persons, one male and one female, in a series of compromising positions, taken from rather close, a bit out of focus. On one of the photos, I could see enough of the woman's face to be sure that it was, in fact, the young Abigail. The man never turned his face toward the camera, but the curls that almost reached his shoulders were pale against her naked skin and couldn't be more different from the cropped dark hair of Anthony in their wedding photo. I imagined that she would have some explaining to do if the baby turned out to favor its actual father.

I untied the lilac ribbon and glanced through a couple of the letters. They were indeed love letters, and with a healthy dose of lust on every page as well. There seemed to be a blend of recounted memories of their previous encounters and promises of pleasures yet unexperienced. Despite the poor quality of the photos, the images were clear in what had been going on, and I couldn't help but envy her a little. If I'd had a passionate encounter like that to remember, perhaps it wouldn't be so bad to be stuck here in this house with an apparently less passionate husband. By all accounts, Anthony was a good man, with a bit of a temper. Perhaps he wasn't as imaginative and uninhibited as the man in these photos, but then … not a lot of men were, I thought, turning one of the photos upside-down and then back again to try and make out which way was up and who was doing what to whom.

I quickly looked through the rest of the letters. They were all similar, apart from the last one. The handwriting was the same as in the love letters, but the contents of the brief note was not titillating in the least.

· · ·

In the morning, I'm off to fight in a war that almost no one believes in, least of all me. The only thing worth fighting for in this world is that space in between your thighs or that soft skin underneath your breasts. Closer to heaven than that, I'll never get, being a sinner at heart.

I'm sending you a small watercolor painting of the view from our hotel balcony in Italy; just a little something to remember me by while I'm gone. On a more serious note, I've made out a will, at the family lawyer's insistence. I'm leaving you all my paintings, if the worst should come to pass ... But don't fret, my loveliest. I'll be back, and when I return, I shall paint you once more in my garden, only this time you'll be wearing nothing but that perfume I bought you in Venice.

Your devoted Laurence

I SAT down on the edge of the bed, staring at the small watercolor painting hanging over the headboard. So that's what that was, the view from the room where these photos might have been taken. It must have been a happy place for both of them, so very beautiful with the calm turquoise waters and the lush greenery surrounding the terracotta-roofed houses.

As I put the letters back inside the hidden compartment, I noticed a single piece of paper in the shadows at the back. I pulled it out and stared at a yellowed and wrinkled old newspaper clipping. It was just a short article with no photo, but the headline made my blood run cold. LOCAL PAINTER DIES IN CAR ACCIDENT, it said. I skimmed the short text and had to bite my lip when I realized what the dry and impersonal words of the article meant. An army truck transporting new recruits to a training camp had swerved to avoid collision with a tractor and overturned in a ditch. Several of the young soldiers had been trapped under the heavy vehicle and a local artist had been reported as dead on arrival at the local hospital. I could barely make out the phrases 'promising talent' and 'young life cut short' as my eyes welled up with tears. It seemed Laurence didn't even make it safely to the war he was supposed to fight in.

I dried a tear that had appeared on my cheek. It seemed they had really loved each other, Abigail and Laurence. It wasn't just a random torrid affair with consequences that had needed to be dealt with. And if Laurence never came back from whatever war he'd been sent to fight in, perhaps it was a good thing that Abigail had found a solid, dependable husband who could give her a home like this. Where she could raise her child, conceived in love, passionate love. It was actually rather romantic.

As long as Anthony never found out that the baby his wife was carrying wasn't his. A man with a temper who discovered something like that … I didn't dare to think about what could have happened to her. A chill came over me, and I looked toward the ceiling, thinking of all the things up in the attic. There were no baby things, not that I'd found so far, and no toys or children's mementos. I wanted to believe that they had lived here, happily ever after, and that they'd had more children, children that were Anthony's, and that he'd loved them all, equally, and that Abigail might have loved her firstborn a little bit more than the others, because of what he or she reminded her of.

I wanted to believe that so much, but there was no evidence to suggest that. Everything I had found pointed in a completely different direction.

21

I PUT the letters back in the secret compartment, and before I closed it carefully, I got the diary from the bed and hid that away as well. As the drawer clicked back into place, I could have sworn that I heard a creak from the landing and I almost jumped out of my skin. I laughed nervously and couldn't help but glance toward the door as I slid the bottom left drawer back in place to hide the keyhole. It must just be the wind picking up, but it almost sounded like footsteps on the stairs. My heart started racing, and I pulled my cardigan closer around me. Silly woman, I admonished myself. There's your punishment for reading other people's diaries and love letters. Now you're going to start seeing ghosts in every corner again. Goodness knows, there were enough corners in this horrible old house. Abigail had good reason to be fearful, with all the secrets that she kept from her husband, but me? What did I have to fear? Nothing. Nothing at all.

It had gone dark outside, and I was quite hungry. I hadn't been taking care of myself properly over the last weeks, and I was starting to feel it, the neglect and hollowed-out feeling of an unloved person. I went downstairs and fixed myself a snack, forcing it down despite the lack of appetite.

Despite my resolve, I kept hearing creaking noises from the hallway, and the hairs on the back of my neck stood up straight. There was no one else in the house; I knew that. I *knew* that. I had never been afraid of ghosts, not even as a child. Why should I start now?

As soon as I'd finished eating, I hurried back upstairs to the bedroom, closing the door tightly behind me. Despite the tension and unresolved issues between Thomas and me lately, I couldn't wait for him to come home. I was even willing to overlook his little fling or whatever it was, if he'd just come home and keep me company during these long, dark evenings that just kept getting longer and darker.

I tucked myself into bed and tried to ignore all the sounds that the house made as the wind from the sea pelted it relentlessly. I tried to distract myself with thinking of Abigail and her lover and those photographs. There was passion there, true passion as I barely remembered what it felt like, and he must have loved her to have left her all his paintings. That's what they were, I suddenly realized, the paintings in the dining room, they were Laurence's and that's why she wanted to cry when Anthony complimented them. It was gutsy of her to hang her lover's paintings in the dining room of her husband's house, but I suppose that she felt the need to hang them somewhere that she'd never forget him. Although, judging by the photos of them, she wouldn't forget him easily.

I tried picturing myself with a faceless lover in a

hotel in Italy, and the fantasy kept me distracted as I slowly fell asleep. But it was a shallow and restless sleep, and as I dreamed that I was lying in my bed, I became uncertain of whether or not I was, in fact, awake or sleeping. The room looked pretty much the same as it had done during the day, apart from a few small details, and there was something about the light that made me realize that this was not actually happening, this was just a dream about something happening here at some other time of day, at some other time of year.

My heart was racing, and I huddled under the covers, pulling them closer around me for protection. Protection from what, I didn't know. What was this? Was it just a dream or was I starting to go mad? Was I awake or asleep? Was this real or was it my imagination?

Suddenly, I saw Abigail, sitting on the chair by the writing desk, hurrying to gather up the photos and love letters and hide them in the secret compartment before the door opened. She glanced around the room, and her eyes widened in panic when she noticed her small diary on the bed behind her. She flew up and hurried over to it, not noticing that one of the photos had been stuck to her sleeve and fluttered to the floor like a leaf in autumn behind her back as she hurried to retrieve the diary. The secret compartment in the desk was already closed, and she looked around for another hiding place. The large armoire was standing against the wall by the door, and she quickly pulled one of the drawers out as far as it could go, tucked the diary behind it and slammed it shut at the very last second.

Suddenly and without warning, the door opened so violently that it slammed against the wall. The small watercolor painting hanging over the bed crashed to the floor right behind me. A man stormed into the room. Anthony. He was tall and striking, just like in the photos in the old album, but even more handsome than the photos had suggested. He was also very, very angry in a seething kind of way. His dark eyes seemed to be glowing, even though the rest of him was barely visible against the backdrop of my bedroom.

He looked around the room, searching for something, and just as the woman shrugged and adjusted her dress in front of the mirror hanging next to the armoire, his eyes fell on the photograph on the floor. She saw in the mirror as he bent over and picked it up and the collected self-control on her face cracked. She turned slowly as he stood up with the photo in his hand, his face twisted in confusion, then in realization and last in humiliation. He turned toward her, and I expected him to hit her, but instead, he just stood there, his fist clenched around the image of his wife's betrayal. I could see his lips move, but they didn't make any noise.

The woman looked away and didn't answer his accusations. Instead, she started to leave the room, her movements slow and rather cumbersome due to her big, round stomach. The man tried to make her stay, but she pushed past him, opened the door and continued out into the hallway. I could see them on the landing outside, as if the bedroom wall had suddenly disappeared, every detail crisp and clear. The man, so angry and so hurt, pointing at the photo, demanding an explanation and the woman just brushing him off, refusing to speak to him. She was walking away from him once again, and he turned his back to her and tore the photo into little pieces that he let fall to the floor before burying his face in his hands. Behind his back, the woman tripped on an upturned corner of the hallway rug. It was only a small stumble, but the fact that she was heavy with child and the proximity to the stairs meant that just one small misstep led to disaster. I didn't hear a sound, but I could picture the scream when I saw the man turn and lunge to try and catch her …

Too late.

I didn't see what happened to the woman but could tell by the look on the man's face that the fall had ended badly. He hurried downstairs, and as he disappeared out of sight, I forced myself to wake up and emerged from the dream with my heart racing and a throbbing headache, trembling from top to toe. The room was dark, once more, and empty. The bed next to me, as well. Thomas had still not come home. I stared at the alarm clock on his nightstand, trying to make sense of the numbers. 9.45 PM. How was that possible? It felt as if I'd slept for 12 hours straight, but at the same time, it felt as if I'd never gone to sleep at all, as if I'd been awake all through the scenes that had taken place right here in this room. It was only a dream, I knew that, but it had felt so very real. Only a dream, I kept repeating to myself. But I had never experienced a dream like that, never ever. I turned and looked at the empty pillow next to me. And where was Thomas? How could he not be home by now?

I rubbed my face and felt the dryness in my mouth and throat. Seeing that pregnant woman fall to her death … I would never forget the look on her face. The annoyance that turned to concern that turned to terror and at last an acceptance, a realization, that this was going to end badly. She had grabbed her stomach, the last thing she did before disappearing out of sight, trying to protect the child, her only child, the memory of a man that she had loved and lost. I felt nauseated even though it had only been a dream and I had to remind myself that this was just my imagination, this wasn't real, this was not what had actually happened, I had just made all of this up.

I then forced myself to get out of bed and walk over to the door, open it and walk down the stairs. I almost expected to find the woman on the landing, neck bent at an unnatural angle, blood on her dress, but there was no one there. Of course not. There never had been. It's not real, I kept telling myself. It was only a dream. Only a nightmare. A very vivid and realistic nightmare. This was not what really happened. In fact, I had no idea what had happened to Abigail and Anthony. For all I knew, they had moved to Paris and lived happily ever after there, raising a brood of *enfants* on crumbling *baguettes* and milky *café au lait*.

Horrid imagination. Dreams shouldn't be so life-like and realistic. They should be obvious in their dreaminess, a jumble of childhood memories and fragments from long-forgotten TV-shows, not horror movies acted out in one's own bedroom.

I staggered down to the kitchen, busying myself with making some tea and trying to find something to eat. I felt hollow, as if I hadn't eaten all day or even all week, and when I thought about it, I couldn't remember when I had last had a proper meal instead of just sand-wiches. No wonder that I felt so weak and that the things I'd read in the diary and those letters had gotten to me like that. I needed to take better care of myself.

But the thought of preparing actual food felt insurmountable, and in the end, I just sat at the small kitchen table, nibbling a piece of bread, trying to clear my head.

It was just my imagination, that was all. Just a bad dream. I clung to that fact, trying to push the haunting images out of my mind. I had been spending too much time alone, with only my depressing thoughts, broken heart and lost hopes to keep me company. And that stupid diary and all the beautiful things left behind in the attic to fuel my romanticized fantasies. I needed to forget about all of that and focus on reality, on what was real. Not Abigail and her unknown destiny. That way madness lies, I told myself and forced down another bite. The bread tasted like cardboard.

22

I NEVER OPENED the secret compartment again. Partly because I was afraid of what would happen if I should read any more. But mostly because it didn't matter, anyway. It didn't matter how it had ended. Abigail's and Anthony's destinies were irrelevant to my life here, now. I needed to focus on practicalities, on pulling down wallpaper and scrubbing the grime off windows, and try to take better care of myself. Fantasizing about strangers when I would never know the truth was meaningless. What was the point of wallowing in another couple's unhappy marriage? Didn't I have enough problems with my own?

But despite my resolve, I couldn't stop thinking about the husband. Anthony. The look in his eyes when he had stormed into the bedroom, desperate for his wife to tell him the truth, perhaps even beg his forgiveness, didn't really mesh with the version of him that I'd gleaned from the pages of the diary. It wasn't pure rage or hatred as I'd expected after having read Abigail's description of him. There had been an infinite sadness there, and I wondered what had made my overactive imagination portray him as if he must have really loved her. There was nothing in Abigail's diary that suggested that he'd been that passionate about her, so why had I conjured that image of him? I didn't know what that would feel like, to see one's wife in such a compromising photo and realizing that the child you've been longing for might not be your own, but I could imagine that it could make a man resolve to violence. But despite the brutal betrayal, he'd never laid a hand on her, just pleaded with her, begged her to stay and to be honest with him. I didn't think that he would have forgiven Abigail, but he might have appreciated the gesture. On some level, at least.

The despair on his face after his wife had plummeted to her death kept haunting me, and I couldn't help but wonder what Thomas would have looked like, had it been me. Of course, he wouldn't have been home to witness my fall, in the first place. He was hardly ever at home anymore, leaving for work at the crack of dawn and returning home long after I had gone to bed alone in the echoing empty house. And if he had been there, the sound from the TV in the bedroom would probably have drowned out my last scream.

I sighed and plunged my hands into the warm and sudsy water, fumbling after the last of the teacups.

When the dishes were done, I dried my hands and stood for a long time, just looking around me. The frantic work over the last few weeks had come to a sudden stop, and I found it impossible to muster any enthusiasm for anything to do with the house. What was the rush? I had no deadline, no place I had to go, nothing to do but fix up this old house. For the rest of my miserable and lonely life.

I looked at the table and noticed that the sun hit the surface in slanted lines through the recently washed windows. The brightness and warmth took me by surprise. I couldn't remember when I had last seen the sun. Could hardly remember what it felt like to be warm. It had been gray and dreary since we had moved here, and the house was constantly drafty and chilly, impossible to heat with its single glazing and lack of insulation. But today the sun was shining from a pale blue sky, and the sea looked calmer. The constant wind seemed to have abated. Perhaps I should go for a walk? It looked surprisingly mild for October, and if it snowed soon, I might be stuck indoors for a good long while. Best take advantage of this lovely day. It might cheer me up. Goodness knows that I needed cheering up!

I went upstairs and put on some warmer clothes before grabbing my coat, some mittens and a scarf from the hall closet and stepping outside on the porch. Despite the enticing blue skies, it was pretty cold, but the sun made it pleasant, and I set off at a good pace along the coast, keeping away from the cliffs that made me uncomfortable and vertiginous. I'd never get used to having them so close.

After making sure that the cows were all the way down the hill by the neighbors' house, I hurried across the field. On the other side was a small copse of trees, leaning inland from the constant winds from the sea. Beyond the trees was a trail that followed the coast, with benches and bins here and there for hikers and tourists. Why anyone would want to spend their holiday in this dreary place, I couldn't imagine, but when I rested for a while on a bench with a stunning panoramic view of the ocean half a mile or so down the coast, I had to admit it had a certain something. Perhaps even charm.

Just as I was thinking about continuing my walk, I heard barking and saw someone coming along the path in the opposite direction. It was an elderly couple, surrounded by three or four small dogs, and I was just about to get up when I recognized the woman.

"Mrs. Kensington!" I exclaimed.

The woman sat down next to me and sighed contentedly, rubbing one of the dogs behind the ear. "Yes?" she said, peering at me against the sun.

"I'm Lisa. Stevenson. We're neighbors."

"Oh, right," the woman exclaimed. "I didn't recognize you there at first. This is my husband," she said and indicated the man that had caught up and came and sat down next to her. "My George. This is her, I was telling you about, dear," she said rather loudly. "Hard of hearing, he is," she added to me in a softer voice. "The one who moved into the house on the cliffs," she belted at her husband.

The man looked me up and down and grunted something that might have been 'hello'.

"I've been meaning to stop by," I said. "I wanted to thank you for the lemon squares and return your cake tin. I've just been so very busy ..."

The woman waved off my apology. "Don't worry about it. I can't even imagine the state of that house after all these years. I'm glad to see you out and about, though. I was afraid that the ghosts might have gotten to you."

Her husband harrumphed, and I laughed, although the laughter sounded a bit hollow after my experiences last night. No, no ghosts. Just my overactive imagination and too much time on my own. Oh, how I needed this. A chat with the neighbors. A walk in the sunshine. Nice, normal activities with nothing supernatural about them.

"No, I haven't even seen any ghosts yet," I said and tried to sound unruffled.

Mrs. Kensington shook her head. "You need to take care," she said and put her hand on my arm. "Especially this time of year."

"Really?" I didn't like the sound of that. "What do you mean?"

"Well, Halloween is coming up, of course. If you've got ghosts in the house, that's when they are the most likely to manifest, you see. They are at their strongest during that holiday; everyone knows that."

I laughed again, but it didn't sound very convincing, even to my own ears. It wasn't that I was afraid of ghosts, but that I knew that winter was coming and I didn't think that the cold and the dark of the winter months would help what was almost certainly the beginning of a depression. I needed to put all these silly thoughts out of my mind, so that I could move on. Return to the present and stay there.

"I wanted to ask …" I began but then faltered when I couldn't think of a good way of putting it.

"About what happened in that house of yours?" said my neighbor, seemingly eager to spill the beans. "Of course. Well, there's all sorts of rumors going around, but as I've heard it, there was a couple who lived there. And the husband went mad, you see. He thought that his wife had been unfaithful, the poor woman, and she was carrying his child, you see, and that made it all so much worse, because he didn't just kill *her.*" The woman grabbed me by the arm and squeezed hard. There was a glint in her eye, of tears, perhaps. "The poor child, you see. It was only weeks away from being born, but perished along with its mother." The old woman shook her head and made the sign of the cross. "Poor innocent little lamb."

I stared at her. It seemed that my imagination hadn't been far off, even though the things I had read in the diary made the husband's madness and the woman's innocence a little less likely. "What happened to the husband?" I asked.

Mrs. Kensington frowned and shook her head. "He got what he deserved," she said and looked out over the ocean. Her husband nodded and grunted something in affirmation. "They hanged him, over at the prison in Westport. And that was that." She turned and looked past me along the path. "That house has been empty ever since. The estate has tried to sell it countless times, but as soon as they hear about the haunting, the buyers all get cold feet."

"The haunting?" I tried to sound skeptical, but my words came out more frightened than questioning.

"Well, he haunts the place, doesn't he?" the woman said, without hesitation. "That madman who killed his wife and baby. He roams the house, in search of his next victim, I've heard that from everyone who has set foot in that house ever since the execution."

I smiled and tried to sound confident when I replied. "Well, I've lived there almost a month now, and no one has tried to kill me." A chill ran along my spine as I said those words. Even though I hadn't met any ghosts, those words weren't entirely true. I remembered Thomas's eyes glaring with hate at me on the stairs. No, of course, he would never have actually killed me, I reassured myself. Of course not. But that man, Anthony, he hadn't actually killed his wife either. Or had he? Was the dream I'd had just my overactive imagination as I'd been trying to convince myself, or was it some kind of trace memories in the house of the tragic events that had taken place there?

"How did he kill her?" I heard myself asking. Oh, please, say that he shot her or strangled her or ran her over with the car, I thought while waiting for my neighbor's answer. Poisoned her with arsenic, anything but—

"Pushed her down the stairs," the old man on the other side of Mrs. Kensington said. "That poor defenseless woman." He shook his head, got up from the bench and started walking along the path.

Mrs. Kensington got up as well. "We must be going. The dogs will be needing their dinner soon. But it was so nice meeting you. And if you should see or hear anything out of the ordinary, you get straight out of that house and come down to us. Any time, night or day, you hear? I couldn't live with myself if anything happened to you."

I forced a smile onto my lips, even though I really felt like bursting into tears. Mr. Kensington's words had hit me hard. Of all the ways to kill someone … How could I have guessed that? Where had that idea come from? "Don't worry, Mrs. Kensington," I said, doing my best to sound calm even though I wanted to plead with them to let me go home with them, to please save me from that house that was slowly but surely driving me mad. "I'm sure there is no reason for concern. But I'll stop by one day, with your cake tin. Thanks again, by the way."

Mrs. Kensington patted me on the shoulder and hurried after her husband, the dogs running back and forth between them. I sat a little while longer on the bench looking out over the ocean, going over what I had been told and trying to make sense of the panicked jumble in my head. Mrs. Kensington's ghost stories, Abigail's diary, my own overactive imagination. The similarities between Abigail and myself. I wasn't sure anymore of what was real and what I'd just made up.

Hearing that the woman and her child had died from a fall, similar to what had happened in my dream, upset me terribly, of course. But it was the husband's destiny that made it difficult to breathe. If what I had dreamed was true, somehow, then Abigail's and the baby's death had been an accident, and Anthony would have been hanged for a crime he didn't commit. I kept picturing the look on the man's face when he stormed into the bedroom, pleading with his wife to please tell him the truth. That was not the face of a killer. Oh, no, that was the face of a man with a broken heart.

With an ache in my chest, I got up from the bench and walked on trembling legs back along the path toward the house on the cliffs.

23

Stepping back inside the dark house after the brisk walk in the sun, I felt truly afraid for the first time. The vast emptiness felt like a presence, almost larger than that of the characters from my dream. I almost wanted to shout out, "Is there anyone here?" but stopped myself. What if I got a reply? What if Anthony Stewart did haunt this place? His home where he had lived with his young and beautiful wife, pregnant with what he must have thought was their first baby. Had he been happy here? What had triggered his first suspicions? Was it something Abigail said or did? Did Anthony find her diary?

I pulled off my coat and put it back in the hall closet, walked into the kitchen and made a cup of tea that I took with me up to the bedroom. I paused with my hand on the doorknob but when I finally opened the door, the room looked unusually cheerful, lit by the October sun. I walked over to the bed, found the novel I'd been reading, and curled up under a blanket.

I opened the book to the place where I'd stopped reading, removing the fountain pen—Anthony's—that I'd used in lieu of a bookmark. I started skimming the text to find my place and then froze.

Straight across the text on the page was written in thick black letters:

NOTHING LIKE ABIGAIL, **you are nothing like her**

I READ the words over and over, feeling a chill despite the warm sun streaming in through the windows. That was not my handwriting. Those were not my words. So, who had written them? And how?

I slowly picked up the fountain pen with trembling fingers and turned it over. The worn-down gold letters on the side of the casing glinted in the sun.

Anthony Stewart.

Was it his words? It didn't seem possible, but I couldn't think of another explanation. I remembered the last time I sat here reading, how hours had passed, and it had gone dark. I had assumed that I had dozed off, but perhaps ... Perhaps there was another explanation.

I shook my head, feeling stupid. That Mrs. Kensington and her superstitions had gotten to me. Even though I'd spent the best part of a month in this house, all alone most of the time, and hadn't seen a single ghost, I had still let an old woman's tales get me spooked. And in the middle of the day, to top it all. It was the dream, of course. That nightmare. It had gotten me all rattled and I didn't seem to be able to shake the feeling that what I'd seen was somehow what had really happened.

I got up from the bed, walked over to the window and looked out over the ocean, trying to picture Abigail standing in this very spot, waiting for her child to be born. She must have felt the baby move, and I automatically put my hand on my pitifully empty and flat stomach. No, I wasn't exactly like her, even though there were similarities. In some ways, we couldn't be more different. I would never have cheated on Thomas, for instance, even though his increasing amount of overtime made it pretty clear that he didn't feel the same way. And I would never know what it felt like to carry my beloved's child inside of me.

The heartbreak was as raw and brutal as always. You would think that I would get over it, after all these years. But it still hurt more than I thought I could bear. The only difference was that I didn't feel a longing for Thomas to ease my pain nowadays, not like I used to. Since he didn't feel the loss as painfully as I, he was unable to soothe it. And I so desperately needed someone to comfort me right now.

Mrs. Kensington and her ghost stories. I had run into her at the worst possible time. As much as I'd enjoyed our little chat, the confirmation that Abigail had died the way I'd seen it in my dream … That was just too creepy.

But her son … I sighed and couldn't help but smile when I remembered him. He was exactly the type of man I should have chosen. Sweet, kind, and loved kids. The memory of his dimples made my uterus cramp. But no. It was too late for that now. There wouldn't be any second chances, Thomas had made it clear that he wouldn't let me experience that happiness with someone else. And his madness in investing all my money in this dreadful house meant that I would never experience it with him. Although, I was starting to think that I might have had a lucky escape there.

The anger and violence I had seen in Thomas lately was not something I wanted my unborn children to ever have to experience. Perhaps it was better this way. On a rational, reasonable level, I knew that. But my emotions were all over the place and the hunger inside of me, the infernal ticking of my biological clock, was slowly but surely driving me mad.

Perhaps I would end up killing Thomas, be executed for the murder and then haunt this house alongside Anthony Stewart for all eternity? I suddenly pictured the despair on his face and was filled with a strong feeling of compassion and understanding, incredibly vivid for someone I had never met and who had been dead for decades.

I turned around and looked in the mirror hanging on the opposite wall on the other side of the bed. I could see my own reflection, the messy hair and confused and emotional look on my face that was still flushed after the brisk walk. I could see it all so clearly. The patterned wallpaper, the detailed window frames, the curtains from the attic. It probably looked very much like it did when Anthony lived here, and I felt the closeness, the connection that one can sometimes experience with a complete stranger on seeing how many things one had in common.

As I stared into the mirror, my eyes lost focus for a moment, and everything went blurry. When I had blinked a few times, and looked again, something had changed. I could still see myself standing there, by the window. But I was no longer alone.

24

THERE WAS a man in the room, standing right next to me. Even though I had never seen him before, I recognized him, and even though I should have panicked and run from the room, I didn't feel any fear. Just wonder and longing and amazement.

"Anthony?" I whispered.

He lifted his head and looked in the mirror, meeting my stare with a faint smile. I could see straight through him, but there was no doubt in my mind that he was, in fact, standing right beside me, over by the desk, with one hand on the backrest of the chair. I wanted to reach out to him but was afraid to move. I didn't want him to disappear again, not until I had a chance to ask him …

"I need to know," I whispered. "Did you kill her? Did you kill Abigail?"

He seemed to fade away as I spoke but I could see clearly how he looked at me, his dark eyes filled with a haunted sadness that filled me with affection, as he shook his head slowly. Oh, I recognized that inconsolable sadness, I knew exactly how that felt, and I was seized with an urgent need to soothe his pain and perhaps have him soothe mine at the same time. I so wanted to comfort him, light up those eyes, make that darkness disappear from his beautiful face.

"If you didn't kill her," I said, a little louder but immediately lowered my voice when he seemed to almost disappear in front of me. "Then, you were innocent," I whispered. "They hanged an innocent man."

It looked as if he was struggling to stay visible, but I could see his shoulders relaxing, and the relief wiped away the wrinkles from his forehead as he saw that I believed him. There was still so much darkness and pain in his eyes, but his lips curled into a shadow of a smile. I bit my lip to keep from speaking but as I took a step toward him, he instantly faded away and disappeared in the blink of an eye.

I reached for him, pawing the air where he had stood, but he was gone. There was no one in the room, besides me. I paced back and forth, restless, checking the mirror over and over for his reflection. But nothing. I was alone. As always.

I grabbed a blanket, curled up on the bed and stared out the window, cursing myself for scaring him off as the tears started to flow. Even the presence of a ghost was better than this infernal solitude. The sun was setting and it would soon be dark outside, but I doubted that Thomas would be home for hours yet. He would have already eaten, so there was no point in cooking, apart from the fact that I needed to take care of myself. But I didn't want to. I wanted someone else to care for. Someone who needed my love and affection. Someone I could comfort. It was the next best thing to being comforted myself.

I lay back against the pillows, sobbing, facing the door as I listened for the sound of Thomas's car, but the only thing I heard was the wind that had picked up again and the tireless waves. I felt so intensely lonely, like I was the only person in the entire universe. I closed my eyes and listened to the waves hitting the cliffs down below. The creaking of the old house, shifting and settling. My hiccupping sobs, shaking my entire body.

At first, I thought that I had fallen asleep and not heard when Thomas got home, because I was suddenly convinced that there was someone lying next to me. But then I realized how unrealistic it was that I wouldn't have heard the car, or when Thomas unlocked the front door and came up the creaking stairs. He always made a lot of noise, regardless if I'd gone to bed or not. No way I would have slept through that. Also, whoever was lying on the bed behind me, hadn't reached for the remote and switched on the TV. The room was completely dark, with no flickering lights from the muted TV-screen. That was a dead giveaway.

I held my breath, waiting. What was happening? And what would happen if I turned around? I wanted so much to turn around, but at the same time, I was afraid that I would scare it, him, whatever this was, away if I did. I stayed still, moving as little as I could, taking shallow breaths, focusing on the connection. The tangible closeness.

I could feel a strong presence, but at the same time, there was no body heat and no sounds coming from whoever that was. Whatever it was, it didn't scare me. It felt strangely calming, when it ought to have freaked me out.

A light sensation, like a feather-light caress over my

cheek, made all the hairs on my arms stand up. The feeling was electrifying and made my entire body tingle. Parts of me that had felt dead and numb came to life, and I was filled with an intense longing for reciprocation. How could I just lie here, letting him touch me?

But what else could I do? If I turned around, he would probably disappear again.

I slowly inched the blanket down around my waist, revealing my right arm that was mostly bare. Nothing happened for a long while, but then the soft strange caresses came back and continued from my cheek down my right arm. I could see the goosebumps spreading, but it was an entirely pleasurable experience. I wasn't afraid anymore.

My tears dried on my cheeks as I lay there, feeling the comforting presence in the dark room for what felt like an eternity, until I heard Thomas's car coming up the driveway. As it approached, the soft touches stopped, and I could almost feel something shifting on the bed behind me. "Anthony," I whispered, hoping that he could hear me. "Thank you."

The car door slammed shut outside, and I suddenly knew that I was completely alone in the room. Anthony was gone.

OVER THE NEXT FEW DAYS, I kept working on the house. Not because I cared so much about what it looked like, but because I needed something to do with all my time. It wasn't the frenetic work from the last week or so, though. I took my time and made sure to take long breaks when I sat looking out the window with a cup of tea. It felt as if I was waiting for something, and after a couple of days, I realized what it was. I was waiting for Anthony to come back.

His presence in the bedroom had been an intensely emotional experience; an awakening that had reminded me of what my body was capable of. What it was meant to do. I had felt so numb and empty for so long that it had become the norm, but that was not who I was, deep inside. I longed to repeat the experience, hungered for those emotions to return to my hollowed-out body, and also hoped for a chance to soothe his despair as he had soothed mine. And even if he wouldn't let me touch him —or if he couldn't—I selfishly hoped that he would come back to me again. I hungered for his touch, for the urges it had triggered, for the closeness I had felt even though he had just barely been in the room with me. The strangely intimate feeling made it painfully obvious that I had nothing like that in my marriage. No passion, no intimacy, no connection. Thomas was no longer interested in me. He no longer pulled me closer in bed, just turned his back toward me as soon as he had crawled under the covers and went to sleep. At first, I had felt hurt, but now … I didn't care anymore. I knew he couldn't give me what I longed for, all those days I spent there alone in that big and empty house.

I longed for something that gave me goosebumps and made my whole body tingle. Something that made me feel alive again. And I knew who could do that.

One morning, I woke up to the sound of Thomas's car door slamming shut and him driving off. The last thing I had heard before I fell asleep the night before had been him coming home. Now he didn't even stay in the house long enough for us to meet. That was not a sign of a healthy relationship, I thought and got out of bed, already in a bad mood even though I hadn't even had breakfast yet. The house was freezing, and when I looked out the window, I could see frost roses on the window panes. How on earth would we ever survive winter in this house? It was only the end of October, and I feared that the coming months would be much worse than this.

I pulled on my robe and hurried out into the bath-room, where it was slightly warmer after Thomas's shower. I turned on the shower and took off my clothes quickly, eager to step under the warm water. My entire body felt stiff and frozen and … unloved was probably the word I was looking for. Not only hollow on the inside, as I had felt so often during the last few years, but unloved and untouched on the outside, as well. I once again resolved to take better care of myself and took my time in the shower, lathering my entire body and massaging my scalp thoroughly when I washed my hair.

When I finally stepped out of the large claw-foot tub, the bathroom was filled with steam and warm enough that I didn't need to hurry back into my robe. It was the first time in weeks that I had felt warm and relaxed, and I took my time, rubbing lotion all over my body, trying to care for myself in a way that no one else did.

When I reached over the vast sink to rub the fog off the mirror, there was a movement behind me. I jumped at first, but as soon as I saw his eyes looking back at me in the mirror, I relaxed and smiled. I didn't even feel embarrassed about the fact that I was buck naked. There was, after all, no one else in the room! I forced myself to not turn around and just stared at his beautiful face in the mirror. He stared back, his intensely sad eyes dark and desolate in the foggy bathroom mirror. He was still transparent, but I thought that he looked a bit more solid this morning. Perhaps it was just the different lighting in here, or the steam from the hot shower. Or maybe it was true, what Mrs. Kensington had said, that ghosts were stronger around Halloween. That they could manifest, whatever that meant.

I felt excited at the thought of what he might look like in a few days' time. What his touches might feel like. I blushed and felt silly. How lonely must a woman be if she hungered after some phantom's caresses? I kept eye contact with him. When I opened my mouth to speak, he shook his head and raised one finger to his lips. I nodded silently, and he gave me the saddest smile I had ever seen. It was so beautiful, and I ached inside to be able to soothe his suffering, anyway I could. I had to bite my lip not to burst out into questions or reassurances. No speaking. This was torture.

Then he stepped closer, and I realized that there was more than one kind of torture. His presence in the small room was even more powerful than that time in the bedroom, and I shivered in anticipation even before he had lifted his hand.

The caress started on my shoulder, right at the base of my neck, underneath my hair that was still wet and tangled from the shower. His touch, barely solid enough that I could feel it, moved down my shoulder blade, stopped for a second at the dip of my waist and then continued over the curve of the hip until it left my skin.

The whole time our eyes were meeting in the mirror. I couldn't take my eyes off him, couldn't have moved out of the way if I had tried. This was the most intense experience I had ever had, and it in no way satisfied my longing for affection. It just stimulated my appetite for more.

He touched me again, on the other side this time, a ghostly caress down my body mirroring the previous. I shivered, despite the warmth from the shower, and felt my whole body responding even though he only just barely touched me. Even though he was barely there.

His hand stopped on my hip, and I could see him moving even closer in the mirror until he was right behind me. I felt the other hand land at my waist, and both hands move around my front, slowly but without hesitation, without asking permission. Our constant eye contact was all the consent he needed. One hand moved up to cup my breast, the nipple already standing to attention even before he got close. The other hand moved downward, over my hip and lower stomach, smoothing over my soft curls and disappearing in between my legs.

Even though he wasn't entirely solid, the electric sensation made his touch strong enough to make me gasp for air and grab the sink in front of me. I could feel the rest of his body behind me, not as an actual male body but more as a presence that enveloped me and comforted me. At least until I moved further back to get even closer and felt the unmistakable sensation of his longing against my buttocks. I couldn't stay quiet, a desperate moan escaped from my lips, and immediately I could see his shape behind me in the mirror start to fade away.

"No," I gasped, "oh, Anthony … Please …"

His touch was feeling lighter and less present for every second, but before he vanished completely, I saw him bend down and kiss the side of my neck, slowly and intently. He grabbed my stiff nipple and pinched it hard at the same time as he slipped two fingers inside of me and found just the right spot. I closed my eyes and gave in to the intense emotions, focusing on his touches, the intimacy of his closeness, the electricity of his movements over my body. I came almost instantly, the pent-up energy of weeks and months eager to get some release, and felt my muscles contract around the semi-solid shape of his fingers while I gave out a desperate moan. "Oh, Anthony!"

When I opened my eyes, he was gone.

THE REST of the day I walked around with a contented smile on my lips, humming to myself as I continued with the endless list of tasks needed to get the house in order. I scraped off peeling paint from the banister in the hallway all morning and spent the afternoon sorting out anything useful from the piles of debris in the basement; decades' worth of old household stuff, dried-out tins of paint, gardening tools with broken handles, furniture that needed repairs or a new coat of paint, ugly vases and decorations—probably gifts that might need to be brought out for a visit and couldn't be thrown away—and the day's second positive surprise: several stunningly beautiful candelabras of different sizes, enough to light up a church.

It was arduous work, but the treasures I found and the good mood I was in were enough that I didn't even flinch at the cobwebs when they stuck to my face or jump when I heard scurrying in the corners in the semi-darkness of the basement.

I kept looking for Anthony, constantly keeping an

eye out for mirrors or other reflective surfaces that could give him away. Even though I couldn't see him, I imagined that he was watching me, and so I became more conscious of my movements and how I looked. Instead of putting my hair up in a messy ponytail, I had used some bobby pins to create a practical but still rather flattering hairstyle that would keep my messy curls out of the way while I was working. There was no point in dressing up for this dirty work, but I started planning what I would wear later this evening, after I had washed off all the dust from down here.

At dinnertime, I still hadn't seen him, and I took another shower, fixing my hair again and putting on a pretty dress instead of just slouching around the house in my yoga pants as I usually did. I made some food, actual food, and served it properly on a plate and with a glass of wine. Sitting down at the large table in the dining room, I felt a bit silly. This was exactly the reason why I hadn't bothered to cook lately. It felt so pathetic sitting down to dinner all alone. Thomas probably wouldn't be home for hours, and anyway, it wasn't Thomas that I was missing. As soon as I had thought that, I felt a pang. Please, Lisa, I thought to myself. Tell me that you're not sitting here pining for a ghost!

And no, I probably wasn't. I looked over at the empty chair on the other side of the table and thought about who I wished were sitting there. Not Thomas. Not Anthony. But a husband. Yes, I wanted a husband. Someone who would love me forever. And someone who made me feel the way Anthony did. Not scared and intimidated like Thomas did. But passionate and alive, like Anthony did. Ironic, since he wasn't particularly alive, himself.

As I was finishing up the meal, there was a knock on the door. I put my silverware down on the plate and walked out into the hallway, pulling the curtain on the small window by the door to the side to check who it was. The outside light was off, and I reached for the switch.

A mass of blond curls turned toward me as soon as the lights came on. Blond curls and a wide smile when he saw me.

"Mrs. Stevenson," he said and waved. "It's me, Freddy Kensington. We met a while back, with my mother."

I turned the deadbolt and opened the door. "Hello. Yes, I remember. But please call me Lisa."

He took a step back, probably to seem less intimidating, I realized, and was touched by the gesture. "Me and the kids are staying with my parents over the holiday," he explained. "They're off from school and my ex …" His words faded out and he made an impatient gesture. "Anyway, I wanted to ask you a favor …" He shrugged and looked a bit embarrassed. "My oldest, Timmy, he's eight, and he got a bit upset when he realized that there was nowhere he could go trick-or-treating on Sunday." He smiled the most adorable smile and my heart just melted. "So, I was wondering … If you wouldn't mind …" He bent down and picked up a grocery bag that I hadn't noticed on the porch by his feet. "I bought some candy …" He looked in the bag and then up at me, almost pleadingly. "Would it be terribly inconvenient if I left this bag here with you, and then, on Sunday, if we could just stop by, sometime after dinner, not too late … Bridget is only three and passes out like a light about a quarter to eight …" He seemed to realize that he had drifted off the subject. "If we could just stop by, real quick, knock on your door, and you could just give them the candy?" He held out the bag toward me. "We would be out of your hair in no time, I promise. Only … if you could pretend to be a little impressed by their costumes? It would mean the world to them." He lowered the bag. "It's almost the trickiest part, getting through the holidays for the first time after the divorce," he said looking absolutely helpless and totally adorable at the same time. "Before you've gotten the hang of it, on your own, you know?"

No, I didn't know, actually. But the fact that this man would go to so much trouble for his kids, when he could have just given them the bag of candy and told them to deal with it … That was so sweet of him.

"Of course. I'll be here all night, you can stop by anytime," I said. He held out the bag toward me, and I took it, almost staggering under the weight. "Oh, my. Do you want me to give them all of this?"

He smiled apologetically. "No, perhaps not. I might have gotten a bit carried away. And my mom had already bought a bunch of stuff, so … But are you sure that it's not too much trouble?"

"No trouble at all," I assured him. "It will be fun. I wasn't expecting trick-or-treaters, so it was good that you brought your own candy." I put the bag down by the door. "I'll see if I can get a pumpkin or something to decorate the porch with …" I looked around. "Except that this place probably doesn't need much to transform it into a haunted house."

He laughed, and I laughed with him. It was a beautiful sound, and I felt the remainder of the warmth from this morning ignite once again into a strong flame. He really was a wonderful man. And a loving father. I couldn't help but check out his hands—strong and with long, slender fingers, like a piano player—and imagine what they would feel like, roaming my body in a similar manner to what Anthony had done this morning.

Oh, my. Feeling my body react to the vivid images that flashed through my mind, I wondered if perhaps Thomas was right, after all. Perhaps I *was* a wanton whore, who would throw myself at any man that came along.

"It's a great house," he said, taking another step back and looking up at the facade. "I've always wanted to live here. I imagine it must be amazing to live right by the sea, and in such an old and beautiful building."

I nodded. Not that I had ever thought of this house as beautiful. And the proximity to water had only scared me, up until now. But seeing the house through Freddie's eyes, I could see, sort of, that it was a pretty impressive place. Or, it could be. "Yes," I said, not trusting my voice to say much more.

He took another step back and raised his hand to wave goodbye. "Well, I'll see you on Sunday then. And thank you so much for doing this. It's going to mean a lot to the kids."

"It's entirely my pleasure. I'm looking forward to it," I assured him. And it was actually true.

As he walked back to his car, I stood in the doorway and immediately begun to plan all the things that I needed to do before Sunday. If those kids of his only had one house to go trick-or-treating in, then it had better be the best haunted house in the neighborhood.

When Freddie Kensington had driven off, I closed the door and walked back into the dining room. The food was cold, but I took my wine glass and brought it with me through the rooms downstairs, planning where I should put decorations with a smile on my face. This feeling of anticipation … I had never been much of a Halloween person, but the thought of those children turning up here, hoping for some candy and getting the thrill of their short lifetimes! Oh, I so wanted to make this a special occasion for them.

Picturing the appreciative smile I might get from their father wasn't entirely unpleasant either. I paused on the stairs, looking back at the front door, remembering every detail about him. Those soft curls, the long, slender fingers, the broad shoulders. He was not as tall as Thomas—or Anthony for that matter—but was more powerfully built. He probably worked out. Oh, he could probably give me a real workout, I thought to myself with a smile and kept walking up the stairs.

The bedroom was dark and cold but when I switched on the light by the bed, the small lamp with a red fringed lampshade that I had found in the attic, the whole room seemed to glow. I found my phone, put on some music and danced slowly around the room with my wine glass in my hand, remembering this morning and the visit this evening and then combining the memories into a pleasant daydream about possible future encounters. Of course, any future with Freddie Kensington was out of the question. Thomas was never going to give me a divorce and Freddie was a much too nice guy to want to have an affair with a married woman. But Thomas couldn't keep me from Anthony. Even if he kept me trapped here for all eternity, I would never need to feel alone again.

I smiled and twirled around to the music, stopping immediately when I saw him there in front of me. Oh, he was so very handsome. Not muscular like Freddie, but tall and wiry in a way that was very imposing. I could understand how a jury could have convicted him of murder. There was something so forceful about him, like he had a special energy source inside that made it possible to just carry on, forever. And in a way, wasn't that exactly what he was doing?

The look in his eyes was still intensely sad and despairing, but there was a glint of something else as well, something smoldering with heat in the chilly space. I put the wine glass down on the writing desk and moved closer. He just stood there, watching me. I could still see the room behind him, but could swear that he looked even more solid than this morning. Definitely more present.

I reached one arm behind my back and pulled down the zipper slowly. He watched me intently, as I let the dress slide to the floor and stood there in my cute underwear, that I hadn't worn for ages. It looked as if he enjoyed the view. I walked over to the bed and crawled on top of the covers, not wanting to shield my body from him. The room might be cold, but the look he gave me made my whole body feel on fire.

He just stood there, in the middle of the floor, as I started caressing my body, moving my hands over the soft skin to all the right places where I hoped that he would touch me too. The room was so silent that my breathing almost echoed and even though I let a couple of moans slip out, Anthony didn't fade away.

After a while, I let one of the shoulder straps on my bra slide down and revealed my left breast, the nipple hard in anticipation already. At last, Anthony started to move toward me. He came all the way over to the bed and bent over my almost naked body. He didn't even have to touch me for my entire body to start tingling. I wanted him to kiss me, to caress me, to lay down on top of me and push my legs apart with his body weight, but of course, he didn't have any body at all and no weight either.

I spread my legs on my own accord and felt the energy surrounding him tickling the skin on the inside of my thighs and on my naked breast. He was hovering above me, looking down on me like a lover would, but not really making any move apart from those same feather-like caresses here and there, setting my skin on fire.

Pushing my pelvis closer to him, I felt the tingles in all the right places and soon started panting harder, hoping that he would touch me again. But even though I could feel his desire toward me, he didn't come close enough, and when I reached for him, my hand went straight through.

He bent closer and started placing light kisses along the side of my face and down my neck. Each touch sent a tingling sensation throughout my entire body. When I couldn't touch him, I started to caress myself instead and slid one hand underneath my panties as his electrifying kisses reached my bare breasts. The sensation was unlike anything I had ever experienced, and even though I ached to feel him entirely inside of me, I was soon feeling the staggering tension that would lead to another intense release. Halloween was the day after tomorrow. Perhaps then, he would be able to …

I pictured Anthony coming to me, completely manifest, a solid body aching for the release that only I could give him and the image fused with other memories of today and his fingers became Freddie's fingers exploring my naked skin and the hair I gripped when he kissed my naked stomach wasn't dark and straight but soft blond curls and the longing inside of me was for something so much more than just physical release, I wanted love, I wanted a life, I wanted to be that man's wife, I wanted to be the mother of his curly-haired children, I wanted to live happily ever after here by the sea and fill this haunted and empty house with life and laughter and joy and love and …

I came so hard that I think I might have passed out for a while, my entire body cramping and convulsing from head to toe, screaming out my longing and frustrations at the top of my lungs. The tingling sensation of Anthony's presence immediately disappeared, and I lay there in the soft red glow from the bedside lamp, feeling the chill of the room against my sweating, naked skin. Feeling the emptiness of the room, of the house, against the longing in my heart.

By the time Thomas came home, I was already asleep.

2 8

THE NEXT MORNING, I slept late, and by the time I had dragged myself out of bed and downstairs to the kitchen, Thomas was already dressed and sitting at the kitchen table with a cup of coffee and a displeased frown.

"How much wine did you have to drink last night?" was the first thing he said as I came in through the door.

"Just one glass with dinner," I said and fumbled for the coffee pot. That might be technically true, but it felt as if I had finished off the whole bottle. My head was throbbing, and the rest of my body was sore, as if I'd had a serious workout the day before. Which, in a way, I had. Twice.

I sat down at the table, clutching my coffee mug and letting the warmth spread to my hands.

Thomas looked disapproving. "It didn't seem like just the one glass." He glanced over at the bottle on the counter. It was still almost full. "You were dead to the world when I got back and this morning too."

I took a careful sip of the hot beverage. "I think I

might be coming down with something," I mumbled. "I'm feeling very tired, still."

He looked alarmed. "Well, keep your bugs to yourself, if you don't mind. I've got that important presentation in Portland on Monday morning, and the last thing I need is a cold."

"Portland?" That was the first I had heard of it.

"Yes." He looked annoyed. "You know this. I've told you, ages ago."

"Oh."

"Anyway, since the presentation is so early in the morning, I'm flying out tomorrow morning. I want to have some time at the hotel for the last preparations and be sure to get a good night's sleep."

"But tomorrow is Halloween."

He snorted. "So? The world doesn't stop because of some kids' candy cravings. Some of us have work to do."

"Oh."

I hoped that I sounded disappointed enough, but in reality, I was thrilled to hear that Thomas wasn't going to be home for Halloween. That meant that I could go all out with the decorations and preparations for the trick-or-treating. I took another sip of the coffee and started to perk up.

THOMAS SPENT the entire day planning his important presentation, spreading out tons of paper over the dining room table and staring at his laptop, mumbling to himself now and then.

I did my usual chores and then started pulling things up from the basement or down from the attic to set the stage for the children tomorrow. I cleaned out our entire supply of candles and made a jack-o-lantern for the porch out of the pumpkin that Thomas had brought home so that I could make him a pie.

Dinner was a strained event, with Thomas constantly glancing over to his stacks of paper that he had only pushed to the side, and several times dropping his fork to reach over and make a note of something as soon as he thought of it.

After dinner, he went back to work, and it wasn't until he was on his way up to bed that he realized what I had been doing all afternoon.

"Are you expecting company?" he said, as he walked through the heavily decorated hallway, and the tone of suspicion in his voice was obvious.

"It's Halloween tomorrow," I explained.

He stopped at the foot of the stairs, fingering the ancient lace curtains, complete with authentic tears and cobwebs, that I'd found in the basement and hung along the railing. He looked at me with a disgusted frown. "So?"

"So, trick-or-treat," I said and walked past him upstairs.

He followed me up to the bedroom. "There won't be any trick-or-treaters out here," he said. "Thank goodness."

"Actually," I said, coming back from the bathroom in my pajamas. "Mrs. Kensington from down the road— the woman who made those lemon bars—her grand-children are here for the holiday, and I said that they were welcome to come here for some candy."

Thomas frowned. "I don't want to find the whole house covered in toilet paper when I get back."

"Don't be silly. They are too small for pranks. I think

the oldest was eight and the youngest three. It'll be fun. I can't wait to see their costumes."

His disapproving frown didn't fade. "Well, I'm glad I won't be here. Such a meaningless holiday. Parents spend a fortune on horrible costumes, just so that children can extort the neighbors and eat so much candy that they make themselves sick."

I pulled back the covers and crawled into bed. "Well, Mrs. Kensington even bought the candy, so there's no trouble at all for us. I'm happy to let them come here."

Thomas slid into bed next to me. "Well, it's a good thing I'm not here then." He looked at me. "I don't understand why you're getting so worked up about this." His eyes narrowed into a suspicious look. "This wouldn't have anything to do with that son of hers? Is that why you planned this? So that you could meet while I was away?"

"I didn't even know you were going away until today," I said. "And no, I'm not planning any secret rendezvous with Mrs. Kensington's son while you're away." I turned my back to him and pulled the covers up.

He didn't say anything more, but I could feel his disapproval and suspicions. Well, it was true. I wasn't planning to get together with Freddie.

But with Thomas away all night, I had great hopes for an intense rendezvous with Anthony.

THOMAS WAS UP EARLY, seemingly eager to get away, but he must have noticed that I wasn't exactly sorry to see him go and as it became time for him to leave, I looked up and saw him standing in the doorway, staring at me.

I had arranged the candy Freddie had brought in a variety of bowls and tureens that I had found in the attic, and with the old lace table cloth and the massive candelabra behind, it looked exactly like something I would have loved to see when I was trick-or-treating as a child.

I could already picture it in my head, even though the hallway was quite bright in the daytime. No lights on, just the candles. The creaks in the floorboards as they walked over to the small table to choose their favorite candy. The wide stairs stretching up into the darkness above and the sounds of rattling window panes and the relentless waves against the cliffs below. It was going to be so scary! The kids were going to love it! The smile on my face must have been radiant, but when I turned around and noticed Thomas standing there, it went out like a light. His disapproving frown deepened.

"If I didn't know better, I would think you had a hot date tonight," he said, and his words cut me like glass.

I forced myself to meet his stern stare. "I do," I said, gathering the empty candy packaging and walking past him into the kitchen to throw it out. "With three small children. This is the only house where they can go trick-or-treating, and I want them to get the complete Halloween experience." I opened the cupboard beneath the sink and threw away the trash. When I stood up and turned around, Thomas was standing right behind me.

"Three children," he said slowly. "And their dad …"

I shook my head. "Stop it," I said. "I've met Mrs. Kensington's son exactly twice, for a total of probably three minutes each time. I'm doing this for the kids. I want them to have a great time." I tried not to let his proximity freak me out. This was my husband, for goodness sake. He was supposed to give me goose-bumps, but in a good way.

"M-hm," he said, skeptically, still scrutinizing my face, searching for signs of a guilty conscience.

"When will you be back from Portland?" I asked and refrained from asking the more obvious questions, such as 'Who are you going there with?' and 'How long have you been sleeping with her?'.

He slowly stepped away and moved toward the door. "I'm not sure. It depends on how the presentation goes. But not before Monday night."

I nodded. "Ok. Have a safe flight. And break a leg with the presentation."

He didn't reply, just nodded curtly. And then he left.

I stood by the small window beside the door,

watching him drive away. Perhaps it should worry me that he went away and took the car. He hadn't asked me to drive him to the airport, so it couldn't have occurred to him that he left me pretty stranded out here with no means of transportation. Or perhaps it had.

Well, if he was trying to keep me from seeing all the men he was convinced I was sleeping around with, he could have nailed the door shut, for all the good it would do him, I thought to myself and walked upstairs.

I took a long bath, hoping that Anthony would show up, but since I was expecting company, I wasn't too disappointed when he didn't. I put on some makeup and did my hair, but when I stood in the walk-in closet, running my flashlight over all the hangers, I couldn't find a thing to wear. Then, I had an idea. I hurried up the stairs to the attic and over to the armoire. The dresses had been hanging there for decades, and I was certain that they would be moldy and smelly, but when I pulled them out into the light, the only thing I could smell was a faint trace of perfume. I brought them back down to the bedroom and tried them on in front of the mirror.

They all fit mysteriously well, but as soon as I put on the black one, I knew that it was the right one for this occasion. It was a classic black dress, form-fitting without looking cheap and leaving my pale arms bare. The light powder and foundation I had used made me look like someone from another time. Like someone else. Perfect. I was in the mood for some playacting tonight.

I went downstairs and prepared some dinner, setting the table in the dining room with fine china and pouring myself a glass of wine that I sipped all through the meal. I had almost set a plate for Anthony but stopped myself. I did pretend that he was there, though, and told him at length about my plans for the trick-or-treaters, even though I didn't see any trace of him. I told him about my own Halloween memories from when I was a child, about the different costumes I had worn and that year when my mom had read an article about someone who had put razor blades in candied apples and cut all my candy into small pieces before she let me eat any of it.

While I ate, the sun set, and as I finished off the last of the wine in my glass, I heard a car coming up the drive. Oh no! I had wanted to make an entrance from upstairs when they rang the doorbell. I had pulled the curtain in the window by the door all the way to one side so that they would see me walking down the stairs, a ghostly figure in candlelight.

I scrambled out into the hallway, lit the candles with fingers that were trembling with excitement and then hurried up the stairs and out of sight. My heart was beating as I listened for their steps on the porch and suddenly I felt someone close behind me. Anthony! I was about to turn around when he grabbed me, hard, from behind and kissed me intensely on the neck. I gasped for air, feeling my entire body respond. Oh, Anthony, this was so not the time, but oh my goodness! He felt so real. So completely solid, as if a living, breathing man had snuck up on me. And speaking about solid … I wasn't the only one who was looking forward to tonight! I pushed my bottom against him and allowed myself a moment of euphoric anticipation. Oh, this was going to be some night!

The knock on the door brought me back to the present. I had company. I pulled away from Anthony's embrace and started walking down the stairs, slowly and dignified, or as dignified as I could, considering my legs were trembling and my heart was racing. I only made it far enough down the stairs that I was visible from the front door where I could see a small child peering in through the window with large, wondrous eyes, before I felt those strong arms grabbing me again. I was just about to protest when I realized that it wasn't just about him being solid in more ways than one. Glancing down, I couldn't see his arms even though they were holding me in a firm grip so that my feet were hovering several inches above the stairs. I looked toward the door when it suddenly opened, slowly on still un-oiled screeching hinges without anyone touching it.

Anthony moved slowly down the stairs but stopped a few steps up, so that my hovering feet were just in the children's line of sight. Those large, round eyes widened even more, and when I glanced at Freddie standing behind his two oldest children with the little one on his arm, his face was also filled with amazement. My heart started glowing when I saw him standing there with his children, completely absorbed in the moment and enjoying this as much as they did.

"T-t-trick or t-treat!" the two older children said in chorus, and the little girl on Freddie's arm echoed them hesitantly a few beats after. "Twick ow tweet?" She had a firm grip on her dad's jacket collar, and her face was a perfect blend of terror and thrill, completely confident in the fact that her dad would never let any ghosts or monsters do her any harm. I felt tears welling up in my eyes and had to swallow hard before I could answer them.

"How about a ..." I was supposed to say 'treat', of course I was, but then I felt my feet slowly landing on the stairs and realized that Anthony wanted to play! This could be fun.

"... trick!" I said and raised my hand to point at the table where all the candy was placed. When I saw the children's jaws drop, I turned my head and looked to my right. A couple of the larger bowls of candy had lifted from the table and was moving toward the door, seemingly of their own volition. I struggled to keep a straight face when I saw the pure amazement on the children's faces. And their dad's too. Freddie was loving this, and I loved him for that.

The bowls hovered in the air, and the children glanced at their dad first, to check if it was all right, before they reached out their small hands to pick a piece of candy. They each had an orange plastic pumpkin-shaped bucket that they dropped the candy bars in and before they knew it, candy was flying from the two bowls and landed in their buckets. The little girl started laughing first and then her two older brothers joined in. Last came Freddie's booming laugh.

When the candy bowls were empty, they fell to the floor with a loud clanging noise.

"Wow!" said Freddie. "That was amazing! How on earth did you do that?"

The enthusiasm and pure joy on his face was the most beautiful thing I had ever seen, and I knew in my heart that he was the one. Oh, I wanted to spend the rest of my days with him and have his children and ...

The fact that I didn't know him, didn't know

anything about him, felt completely irrelevant. I walked down the last few stairs and came over to the door. "Magic," I said, matter-of-factly and shrugged a little, with a sly smile tugging at the corners of my mouth. I looked at the boys—the eldest some sort of Stormtrooper and the middle child a perfect Harry Potter with mended glasses and a lightning-shaped scar that looked like it might have been made with grandma's eyebrow pencil. The little girl on daddy's arm was a fairytale addict, I knew that immediately, but the fact that she had chosen to go as a dragon and not the ubiquitous princess made me instantly fall in love with her. The pink and sparkly purse on her arm was just the perfect complement to her green and padded costume.

"There's some more candy over there," I said, gesturing toward the table. "Help yourselves."

The boys glanced at their dad, and when he nodded encouragingly, they moved slowly over the threshold.

"Bring your sister," Freddie said and put his daughter down on the porch.

"Come on, Bridget," said the oldest and took his sister by the hand.

"I'm not Bwidget," the girl said firmly. "I'm a dwagon!"

The Stormtrooper smiled as if he had heard it a thousand times already. "All right, come on, Dragon. Let's go and see if there are some of those red things that you like."

The girl followed her brothers over to the table, and I was left behind with Freddie by the door.

"Thank you so much," he said. "That was so cool! They're going to remember this for the rest of their lives."

I smiled at him, certain that I would remember this day as well. That I would tell my grandchildren about it. The day when I fell in love with their granddad. "The pleasure was all mine," I said and hoped that he realized that I meant that I wanted to offer him a lifetime of pleasures and joy and magic and treats. Surely, he could read between the lines?

"You have no idea how much this means to me, as well," he continued. "I've missed so many Halloweens with them, because of work, so ..."

"Oh," I said. "What do you do?"

"I'm a police officer," he said.

I nodded. "Plenty to do for you on a holiday like this."

Freddie looked over at his children with pure love in his eyes. I wanted to eat him up. "Yeah, and I've been happy to do it. It's just ... They grow up so fast, you know. In the blink of an eye, they'll be off to college and getting their own families." He turned toward me. "I don't want to miss a minute of it."

I moved a little closer. "Oh, I don't know. I should think you have many more years to enjoy fatherhood." I leaned against the doorstop, feeling the empty space inside of me start to fill up with baby dreams once more. "You're young. Who knows? You might even have more kids someday."

He shook his head. "No, no more kids for me. My wife was adamant that I had a vasectomy after Bridget was born. And I was fine with that. Three is a good number. I'm fine with three."

My heart broke into a million sharp little pieces. Just like that, all those rose-colored dreams vanished. The fact that I had pictured myself pregnant with this man's child, even though I had spent a grand total of fifteen minutes with him, made me feel like a complete idiot. A complete, infertile idiot. Of course, three children were enough. It was more than enough for most people. I would have been over the moon if I had three kids.

The question was, could I be fine with three kids, if they weren't my own? I looked over at the siblings by the table. They looked like fine kids. Great kids. Getting along and helping each other. But they weren't mine. The hollow space inside me echoed. I didn't know if I could be a good wife to a man with three children. Not if I had never been a mom. Never felt the flutter underneath my dress, as Abigail had described it in her diary.

The madness of it all was suddenly so obvious that I blushed and pulled away from him. What was I doing, throwing myself at this poor man? This poor, handsome, wonderful man that had never shown the slightest bit of interest in me? How desperate was I?

Well, pretty desperate. In a couple more years I would be too old to have a child, no matter what the doctors might be able to help me with. I didn't have a minute to waste on a man that couldn't have any more children. Who didn't *want* any more children.

The three Kensington kids had emptied the bowls and came back with their pumpkin buckets filled to the brim. They thanked me profusely and staggered under the weight of their loot back to the car. Freddie thanked me again, and I once again assured him that the pleasure had been all mine. And it had been a treat. But it had also left me feeling intensely sad and in need of some serious comforting.

And I knew exactly what would make me feel better. Or should I say 'who'?

3 0

I CLOSED the door and turned around. The house felt so quiet without the sound of the children's laughter, and the candles had burned down and started to go out, one by one.

Anthony stood on the landing, halfway up the stairs, looking down at me. There was nothing about him that hinted at the fact that he had been dead for decades. The transparency was all gone, and he looked strong and healthy and … like he was in a mood to make me forget all about my sorrows.

Oh, please. Go right ahead, Mr. Stewart.

I walked over to the stairs and started to ascend, slowly, taking my time and using it wisely, letting my eyes wander over his entire body, memorizing the features of his handsome face, the lean body, the long legs. The bulge in his pants that looked to be a very nice piece of manifestation, if you asked me.

I stopped a couple of steps below him on the stairs, putting me at the perfect height. I lifted my hands and while looking him straight in the eye, unbuttoned his trousers, pulled down the zipper and revealed what was inside.

Oh, my. There was no doubt in my mind that there was anything other than solid flesh in that throbbing organ that reached out for me as soon as I had freed it from its restraints. I couldn't help myself. It had been so very long since I had felt any kind of passion in my life and these past few days had been intensely emotional. Getting this opportunity to forget about all my sadness and longing for a few hours in a way that surely must be considered guilt-free and completely without strings was just too appealing. I leaned forward and took him in my mouth, all of him, as far as he would go, and tried to keep from moaning, in case that made him fade away. Oh, please let him not fade away. Not this time. Not now. I needed this so bad right now; I didn't know what I would do with myself if he should just vanish right in front of my eyes.

I moved up and down his straight shaft, over and over, until he grabbed me by the hair at the back of my neck and forced me to stop moving. Ok, so even ghosts do not have limitless stamina. Good to know.

He came down a couple of steps so that we were at eye level and kissed me intensely, so hard that my lips tingled after he had let me go. Then he kept moving further down the stairs, kissing me at every level, on the neck, down my bare arms, until he could slide his hands up my dress and push it up around my hips, out of the way for him to bury his face between my legs.

I tried to grab his hair but it was too short in the back, so I just grabbed him behind the neck and pulled him closer, trying to set his pace. He wouldn't follow my directions, though, but continued at his own speed, which quickly made my knees buckle and I had to sit down. He fell on his knees between my legs and kissed the inside of my thighs all the way back to the soft folds that were spreading for him now that I was sitting.

I lay back on the stairs and just let him do whatever he wanted. Whatever he could think of would be fine with me at this moment. I just wanted to lose myself in these intense physical sensations and not think about what it would be like to see those soft blond curls move in between my thighs …

No, don't think about that. Don't think about anything at all, just feel this, just feel this man going absolutely crazy between your legs, doing everything in his power to make you satisfied.

It didn't take long. All the emotions over the last couple of days had made me intensely sensitive, and that rather worked to my advantage in this situation. I felt my entire body surge with pleasure and an intense release when he pushed me over the top and I screamed out, even though I had been trying my hardest not to.

Fortunately, it didn't seem to affect Anthony the way it had done on the previous occasions, and as if to prove that he was still very much here, he pulled me up from the stairs, lolling like a rag doll with every muscle in my body still soft and mellow from the orgasm, turned me over so that I was standing, wobbly, on all four and rammed his solid organ into me from behind, all the way to the hilt. It should have been too much, but tonight there was no such thing. Just bring it on, I thought, just keep doing that, over and over. I can take it. Oh, I can take this for as long as you can give it.

He pulled back and pushed in again, and again and again. I could feel his hands moving over my body, squeezing my breasts, sliding down my front and starting to rub that special spot to get me back on track again. I didn't think it would be possible, but soon I felt the tension start to build again, and I braced myself for another orgasm. This time he came with me over that cliff, and I felt him convulsing inside of me, in time with my own muscle contractions. It felt amazing, like I wasn't even on the stairs any longer, and when I looked down, I realized that I wasn't. We were floating together a few feet over the solid wood, him still inside of me starting to go soft but still a pleasurable presence.

He kissed the side of my neck slowly and kept caressing my breasts as we moved slowly up the stairs, through the hallway, into the bedroom and over to the bed where we landed softly, still joined. It was perfection. I didn't think I had ever felt such pleasure, such intense emotions, and it was the most perfect timing, to soothe my shattered dreams of motherhood and the grief over my failed marriage. I couldn't think of a better remedy.

He stayed inside me until he began to harden again, caressing me and kissing me the entire time. I guess I should have been tired but my body was wide awake, and when he pulled down the zipper on the back of the dress and eased it over my head to keep our connection, I didn't feel the least bit cold even though the bedroom had been freezing every day since we'd moved in.

He rolled over on his back and pulled me on top of him where I started rocking gently back and forth as I looked down on his perfect features. The despair in his eyes hadn't disappeared, but it was decidedly softened by the desire and arousal. His eyes and hands moved over my naked skin, exploring, caressing, egging me on until I picked up the speed. He pushed himself up off the bed and sat up with me straddling him, riding him as hard as I could while he sucked on first one nipple and then the other. The third orgasm was just as intense as the previous two, and he didn't seem the least bit tired. We floated up in the air again for a bit, just to catch our breath and cuddle a little, but soon he lay me down on the bedspread and pushed inside of me again.

There was something so completely surreal about the entire experience that I just let myself—my *real* self —go and just went with the flow, the intense flow even though I had no idea where it would take me. Where was this going to end? When? How? Would we just keep doing this until one of us disappeared—him—or starved to death—me? I didn't know, and frankly, I didn't care much either. Instead, I just raised my arms and braced myself against the headboard to meet his thrusts with as much strength as I could muster. I was no longer afraid of Anthony disappearing on me if I was too loud, so I let him know exactly how he made me feel, moaning, screaming, laughing when I felt the tension start to rise for another release. I grabbed his taut buttocks and pushed my nails into his firm flesh to take him with me. A few more hard thrusts and I felt him shudder and collapse on top of me. His hard shaft convulsed repeatedly inside of me, and I gripped it firmly with my inner muscles to hold him still.

I never wanted this moment to end. Everything was perfect right now. I felt so good. I had no problems or sorrows or desires beyond those that Anthony had so thoroughly satisfied.

"I knew it," came a hateful voice from the door. "You lying, cheating bitch!"

I turned my head and stared at Thomas standing in the doorway. How long he had been standing there, I had no idea. I hadn't heard the car pull up, but then again, I hadn't heard a thing apart from my own moans and screams for the last few hours, so …

He took a couple of steps into the room. "Who the hell are you and what do you think you are doing with my wife?" He kept moving toward the bed, but just as he reached out to pull Anthony off me, my ghost lover disappeared. I lay on the bedspread, completely naked, legs apart, still reeling from the exertion and the shock of seeing Thomas. When Anthony disappeared right in front of his eyes, Thomas staggered backward toward the door, eyes opening wide, his jaw dropping. "Wha-what the hell w-was that?"

I took the opportunity to scramble out of bed and grab my robe, tying it close around my waist. "What was what?" I said, trying to catch my breath. "I have no idea what you are talking about."

Thomas stared at me. "Where did he go?"

I shook my head. "I have no idea what you're talking about," I said again. "I was asleep, and then you came in and started screaming."

Thomas looked around the room. "I *saw* you," he said, his eyes narrowing. "I saw him … *fucking* you." He turned toward me. "I saw you fucking another man, you lying whore. I knew you had something planned for tonight. That's why I had to come back." He bent down and pulled the bed ruffles to the side to check under the bed for the mystery man. "And I was right."

I pulled the robe tighter around me. "I don't know what you're talking about," I whispered. What else could I say? "There is no one here. Surely you can see that."

He stood back up again, moving closer, his hands curling into tight fists. "I know what I saw," he said, and his voice was dripping with contempt. "My whore wife going at it with another man. In our bed!"

I tried to pull away from him, but there was nowhere to go. I was trapped between the writing desk and the bed and the man that was supposed to love and honor me until death did us part. "I don't know what you're talking about," I repeated, like a retarded parrot, stuck on this one phrase. "There is no one here. I'm all alone."

The blow came out of nowhere, and the first thing I noticed was not the fist coming toward my face but the sensation that the entire left side of my head had exploded in pain. I was thrown sideways by the force of the punch and hit my hip on the writing desk, bending over from the pain. He grabbed me by the hair and pulled me back up again. "Now, I'm asking you again," he said through gritted teeth. "Where did he go?"

"There's no one here …" I managed to force the words out even though I could barely feel my face. "Please, Thomas."

He pulled me closer, grabbing me by the throat with his other hand without releasing my hair. "Don't you 'please, Thomas' me, you lying whore. I saw you. I heard you even before I came inside the house." He bent forward so that his face was right next to mine. "And now you are going to tell me where he went, so that—when I'm done with you—I can kill him too."

I could feel his warm breath on my face and struggled for air. White spots started to appear in front of my eyes, and when I tried to pull away from his grip, he just lifted me higher so that my feet didn't reach the floor enough to get any traction. "You are going to tell me," he whispered. "If it is the last thing you do."

Just as I was about to pass out, I heard Thomas gasp and curse. Then his grip on my throat loosened and I fell to the floor.

I DON'T KNOW how long I was unconscious, but as I slowly came too, it was to the sound of screams. Terrified screams. Thomas's screams, even though I didn't recognize his voice at first. I'd never heard it sound like that. My brain was a foggy mess, and I slowly lifted my head from the hardwood floor and forced myself to open my eyes. The room was dark, and I had trouble focusing. It hurt. Everywhere. Every part of my body wanted nothing more than to lie back down again, to disappear back into the bliss of not being conscious of what was happening.

I grabbed the seat of the chair next to me and managed to pull myself back on my feet. When I raised my head, Thomas was standing in the middle of the floor, arms raised in a boxing stance, staring wildly around him. "Who are you?" he screamed. "What the hell is going on?" It looked as if something pushed him from behind and he turned around and started to throw punches in every direction but not hitting anything. He stumbled forward, as if he had been pushed from behind again and fell toward the bed. I saw that there was nothing between me and the door and knew that I had to get out of here. But my feet wouldn't cooperate, and the floor kept tilting one way or the other. I managed a couple of steps, but then I had to let go of the chair. The distance to the door without something solid to hold on to felt like an impossible feat.

I glanced over at the bed, where Thomas was struggling to get back on his feet, staring in every direction, looking for something, anything, that could explain what had just happened. But there wasn't anything there, and I recognized the panicked look in his eyes when he was forced to admit that there was something going on here that was beyond the realm of reality as he knew it. His eyes were wide with terror and his skin clammy with sweat. Bracing myself, I let go of the chair and threw myself at the door. I heard him screaming behind me but didn't dare to turn my head. Just put one foot in front of the other. Just as I was about to grab hold of the door frame I heard steps behind me and then his arm, his strong arm, was locked around my neck from behind, cutting off my air supply.

I flailed and kicked, but my whole body was already so weak, it didn't feel as if my striking him had any effect at all. He carried me by the neck back inside the room, over to the bed where he pressed me down against the rumpled bed sheets where I only a short while ago had enjoyed the most intense pleasures of my life. Now it appeared that my life was rapidly coming to an end. I gave up trying to pry his arm away from my neck and started fumbling all around me for something, anything that I could use as a weapon.

My fingers knocked against the bed stand, and I

reached for what I suddenly realized was within reach. As Thomas leaned up to my ear, screaming his hateful words at the top of his lungs as if he wanted to make sure that I knew that he was justified in his punishments, I curled my fingers around the thick handle of my massive flashlight and brought it with the last ounce of my strength crashing into my husband's temple. His grip around my neck loosened, but he collapsed on top of me, and his bodyweight kept me pinned down on the bed, gasping for air, tangled in the sheets for what felt like an eternity, before I managed to inch out from under him. I grabbed the edge of the bedframe, pulling myself onto the floor where I landed on one side, my head slamming into the floorboards with a loud thud. I saw stars and thought that I might have to throw up. The room was eerily quiet after Thomas's screaming had stopped, but I could still hear his hateful accusations echoing in my ears as I struggled back on my feet.

Thomas was lying on the bed, staring straight out into the room with unseeing eyes. I didn't need to check his pulse to know that he was dead but it took a while before the full meaning of that word sank in. Thomas was dead. Thomas was dead, and I had killed him.

I looked up and saw Anthony standing on the other side of the bed looking down at my husband.

"Anthony," I whispered. "Oh, Anthony, I've killed him."

My muddled brain was trying to make sense of what had happened and trying to rationalize what I had done, but it failed. I had killed a man, killed my own husband. What if they hanged me, just as they had done with Anthony? At least, I had been guilty. Unlike with Abigail, this had not been an accident. Self-defense, maybe, but still. Thomas was dead. Gone forever. I was swaying from side to side, gasping for air, trying to wrap my mind around what had just happened and failing. Thomas couldn't be dead. He was just here. He was just alive, moments ago. He was just about to kill me and almost succeeding. No, this was not what was supposed to happen tonight. Thomas was supposed to be in Portland. He wasn't supposed to be here. I felt the panic welling up inside of me, as the confusion overmanned the last of my sane reasoning skills at the same time as my energy reserves dropped to almost zero. I couldn't think. I didn't know what to do. I needed to call the police, I needed to turn myself in, I needed to go to jail and pay for what I'd done.

With tears in my eyes, I stared at Anthony on the other side of the bed. He just looked at me with that burning stare, fists still clenched in rage over what had happened. Then he raised his hand and pointed at the door.

"I need to call the police," I mumbled, and started staggering along the bed to get to the other side, to Thomas's nightstand, where the telephone was. I could hardly make out my own words. My mouth felt swollen and bruised, and I must have bit my tongue sometime during the struggle, because I could taste metal.

Anthony shook his head and kept pointing at the door. I could feel that my legs were about to collapse under me, so I nodded and started moving toward the door, grabbing the doorframe as soon as it came within reach. I could call from the extension in the kitchen instead. Good idea. Then I wouldn't have to keep seeing

...

Clinging to the solid wood of the doorframe, I

turned my head and looked back at my husband. He stared straight at me with those empty, unseeing eyes, his face contorted with hate and rage. I shuddered, pushed myself off the door frame and staggered toward the stairs. Hanging on to the railing, I inched my way down the stairs, one step at the time. My head was pounding, and I had trouble seeing straight. A little more than halfway down the stairs the pounding got even more intense, but I felt the last of my energy drain, and after almost falling head-first a couple of times, I had to sit down and wait for the house to stop spinning. I clung to the railing, leaning my head against the wall and closing my eyes, just for a moment. What had I done? Thomas's unseeing stare seemed permanently etched on my retinas, and I couldn't rid myself of that image, no matter how many times I blinked. I had killed a man. My man. My husband. Until death us do part, he'd said, and I didn't know if I ought to laugh or cry when I remembered the way he'd said that. I never believed that he would do me any harm, and I had never in a million years believed that I would be the one walking away from a confrontation like that, if he ever got that violent. Although, I didn't seem to be able to do much walking. I wanted to get up, but my legs didn't want to cooperate, and I felt tears welling up at how utterly helpless I was, just sitting here. I knew I had to do something, downstairs in the kitchen, but had no idea what. It felt important, but I didn't seem to be able to hold on to any particular thought for more than a fraction of a second, before my probably concussed brain jumped to the next idea. What was going to happen to me now? I started to panic, but then I couldn't remember why I needed to worry. I just wanted to go to sleep. I lay back on the stairs, resting my head on the hard wooden steps and the dizziness subsided a bit, but the pounding in my head didn't. In fact, it got even louder. So loud that it almost seemed as if it came from outside my head.

I forced my eyes open, sat up and inched down a few more steps so that I could peer down at the front door. Someone was banging on the door. Before I could figure out what that meant, the banging stopped, and a face appeared in the window next to the door. I had forgotten to pull the curtains shut. Mrs. Kensington looked straight at me and screamed as if she had seen a ghost. Or a murderer. If she only knew. She disappeared from my view, and I heard her shouting something, at the top of her voice, but I couldn't make out the words.

Knowing there was someone there, someone who might be able to help, gave me the strength to carry on. I pulled myself up and inched my way down one step at the time. Before I had made it to the foot of the stairs, Freddie's face appeared in the window. He took one look at me and then pulled out his phone. I staggered toward the front door and fumbled with the bolt. Somehow I managed to unlock the door that opened abruptly since Freddie was pulling on the handle from outside. He caught me as I fell and lifted me up in his arms.

I could hear Mrs. Kensington babble, even though it sounded as if her voice came from a place far away. Something about a blanket in the car. Something about the police. Something about blood. Bruises. Who's blood? What bruises? I had no idea. Freddie carried me off the porch and out into the darkness. His arms held me tight, and I rested my pounding head against his broad chest. It was freezing outside, but someone wrapped something soft around me that smelt decidedly of dogs. Oh, dear Mrs. Kensington.

I felt Freddie put me down on the backseat of a car, tucking the blanket around me and then pulling away.

"Oh, no, Freddie," I heard Mrs. Kensington say. "You are not going in there, and that is final."

"Mom!" His reply sounded more amused than annoyed. "I'm a police officer. What on earth do you think I do all day."

"This is different. That is not just some criminal in there! That house is haunted!" Those last words came out in a loud whisper, as if she didn't want the ghosts to know that she was on to them. If my face hadn't hurt so bad, I would have smiled.

I wanted to tell them what had happened, what I had done, but couldn't make a sound. Croaking yammers was the only thing I could manage, and none of them even turned toward me. "Mom …" he said, and then he turned and walked toward the house, and I saw Mrs. Kensington slap one hand in front of her mouth, with tears in her eyes.

I wanted to tell her that she didn't need to be afraid, that the only killer around here was me and I wasn't strong enough to swat a mosquito at the moment, but it seemed I had forgotten how to create words and form sentences and everything hurt so very bad that I just had to close my eyes for a while.

I heard someone pounding on a door and became confused. Hadn't that happened already? Was I still sitting on the stairs? Oh, no, I needed to go downstairs and open the door. But the reassuring scent of dogs enveloped me, and I decided that I must have imagined it.

"The door was locked," I heard someone say. "He's locked himself in. I'm going to see if I can find another way in."

And then another voice, "Oh, no, you don't. You're not going inside that house without backup."

And then we heard sirens.

I opened one eye enough to see the blinking lights light up the inside of the car where I was lying, snug as a bug in a dog-smelling rug. Voices, several voices, authoritative and taking-charge kind of voices. I tried to sit up, to see what was happening and if there was something I should be doing. I kept thinking that I should tell someone, that I must confess, but the pounding in my head got louder, and the car seemed to tilt over on one side, and before I managed to say anything, everything went dark.

3 2

WHEN I WOKE UP, everything was so bright. White and bright. White and bright and fluffy and light. My head didn't hurt anymore. Nothing hurt. There had been pain, I remembered that much, but now I couldn't even remember what kind of pain it had been or where or even who had felt it. Everything felt numb and relaxed and mellow, and I slowly realized that I must be sedated and on some serious painkillers. The mattress I was lying on felt like marshmallow. The bed was narrow, with railings on both sides, and a drip tube was connecting my left hand with something hanging above me, out of sight. The walls were beige and bare and striped by the faint sunlight coming in through the blinds. To my left, a white curtain was pulled closed around what I assumed was another bed, and I could hear voices coming from the other side.

"Hello?" My voice sounded course, as if I hadn't spoken for days. My throat felt swollen, like I'd been ill.

The curtain was pulled aside with a rattle, and a nurse peeked out. "Well, look who's finally awake." She smiled in a professional manner and walked over and started checking my vitals. "How are you feeling," she asked, taking my pulse with two fingers on my wrist and eyes on her watch.

"Er … fine?" Truth be told, I wasn't feeling much of anything at all at the moment, and after the last few days that wasn't necessarily a bad thing.

"Good," she replied automatically in a manner that suggested that she would have said the same if I had told her that I was in excruciating pain.

"Where … what … wh—" I didn't know where to begin to try and unravel the mess inside my head. It felt as if someone had taken out all the contents of my brain, all my emotions, all the knowledge, memories, and skills, stuffed it in a blender and puréed it before pouring it back in through one ear. And then there was my body, that seemed to have been taken apart and then put back together by someone who didn't know anything about anatomy.

"Someone will be in to speak with you shortly," the nurse said. She made a note of something on my chart and then walked briskly away.

"Wait …"

But she didn't.

I lay there, staring at the shadow shapes on the wall, trying to remember what had happened. Nothing. I couldn't remember a thing. And then suddenly, I could remember everything. All at once. The children's laughter and the flying candy, Anthony going down on me on the stairs, Thomas's fist crushing my face, the blanket that smelled of dog. And the staring. Thomas's eyes staring at me from the bed. His raging screams right by my ear. And the silence that came after them.

The police had come; I was pretty sure of it. They must have gone inside the house. Then they must know what had happened. What was going to happen now? What was going to happen to me?

The door to the room opened, somewhere out of sight behind the curtain surrounding the next bed. I slowly turned my head, not sure who I was hoping it would be.

Freddie Kensington stepped into my line of sight and all the emotions on his face was nothing to the chaos I felt seeing him. Longing, embarrassment, desire, shame. He glanced behind him and stepped closer to the bed.

"I'm not supposed to be in here, but I just had to see …" He looked at my face and shook his head. "Are you ok?"

I didn't know what to say. Of course I wasn't. Not in any way. But scrambling for a response, I realized that he couldn't know what I'd done. He would not be looking at me like that, if he knew. As if he was worried about me. As if he cared.

The tenderness in his eyes almost killed me, as I realized that it would all go away as soon as he found out what I'd done. The pain of knowing that I would never experience him looking at me like that ever again was almost too much, on top of all my injuries. It was just the sedatives that kept me from feeling anything at the moment. "There's something I need to tell you," I croaked.

He took another step closer. "Don't worry about that now," he said. "You just need to concentrate on getting better. Do exactly what the doctor tells you, ok?"

I tried to gather my thoughts and came up with a question. "What were you doing there? At the house?"

He shrugged. "Bridget must have left her purse behind, on the table by the candy. She realized it was gone just as she was going to bed, and went completely hysterical until I told her that I would go and get it. My mother didn't think it was appropriate that I should go there alone, calling on a married woman late at night …" He rolled his eyes. "… so she came along as a chaperone. She went to knock on the door, and when you didn't answer, she peeked in the window and started screaming at me to come." He shook his head. "When I saw you there on the stairs …"

He stared at my face, and I didn't want to imagine what it must look like.

"Thomas …" I whispered. "There's something I need to tell you. It's about Thomas …"

He didn't look me in the eye at first. Just stared at my hand with the drip on the blanket. Then he slowly shook his head and forced himself to look directly at me.

"I'm so sorry," he said. "By the time the police managed to get inside the house … it was too late."

I frowned. "What do you mean? 'Managed to get inside'?"

"The door was locked. He must have followed you downstairs, locking the deadbolt behind you while I took you to the car. When the police arrived, they didn't want to just break the door down, because they didn't know if he was armed, so they had to find another way in. It took a while and …" He bit his lip. "I'm sorry. By the time they got inside, he had already left the house through the back door. There was nothing they could do in the dark; they had to wait until daybreak before they could start the search."

I still didn't understand. Search? What would they need to search for. Thomas had been lying right there, on our bed, and the flashlight I'd hit him with must be somewhere on or nearby the bed. I had no memory of having taken it with me.

"I … I don't know what I did with the flashlight …" I croaked.

Freddie looked almost embarrassed on my behalf when he explained. "I'm sorry, Lisa. The doctor told me that you've got a concussion and that you may suffer some memory loss due to the trauma. I understand that this must be confusing for you, but I still think you should know what has happened. Your husband killed himself last night. He threw himself off the cliffs behind your house."

I just stared at him, my brain flooded with conflicting images. The one that kept coming back to me was Thomas, on our bed, staring at me with empty, dead, eyes. Threw himself off the cliffs? Killed himself? I shook my head, hearing his screamed curses echoing through my concussed skull.

"No, I …" I started, but then the door opened, and the strict nurse reappeared behind Freddie.

"What on earth …? Didn't I tell you lot that Mrs. Stevenson needed to rest?" She ushered Freddie out of sight behind the curtain and out the door, reprimanding him all the way. The door closed behind them, and her voice became a muted, inarticulate melody that I couldn't make out the words to. They must have moved away, because the melody faded and the room went quiet again.

I raised my hand and rubbed my face. It felt strange and rubbery, and most of it was covered with bandages and tape. Everything in my brain was a mess, but I knew one thing for sure. Thomas had not killed himself. I had killed him. And I would have to pay for it.

3 3

THE NEXT FEW days passed by in a blur. The sedation didn't help either. As soon as I started to be able to think straight, they came and gave me another shot, and it was off to dreamland again. Doctors and nurses came and went in the mist, and slowly I started to heal. On the outside, at least. The police came, eventually, but left me with more questions than before.

Thomas had killed himself, they said. An open-and-shut case of suicide. Very tragic. There were reliable witnesses who could testify to the fact that I had been assaulted and that Thomas had locked the door behind me when I fled, before leaving the house through the back door and flinging himself off the vertiginous cliffs onto the sharp rocks below.

He had left a note, apparently, to rule out an accident. At first, they didn't want to tell me what it said, but after debating amongst themselves, they reluctantly asked me to verify that it was my husband's handwriting.

The note was written on a blank page torn from

Abigail's diary, which was strange because the diary had been hidden away in the secret compartment and Thomas hadn't known it existed. It had been written with a black fountain pen that had been left on top of the note. The police officer handed me the torn piece of paper inside a transparent evidence bag.

"We just need you to confirm that this is your husband's handwriting, ma'am."

I stared at the words, the elegant cursive handwriting in perfect lines across the page, nothing like Thomas's messy scrawl.

No man should ever raise his hand, let alone his voice, to the woman he has sworn to love.

Please don't feel guilty about what happened; none of this was your fault. I want you to try and find the happiness that you deserve and hope that you will stay on in this house, in our house, despite everything that has happened. I hope you will be very happy here, and that the happy memories will overshadow the bad ones.

I don't know that my actions make anything right, but I hope this will be the beginning of something new, if not for me then for you.

Remember that love always triumphs over hate. Life over death.

Always, my lovely, always

TEARS WELLED UP, and I slapped one hand in front of my mouth.

"Did your husband write this note, ma'am? Just say yes or no."

I read the words once more, memorizing every line, in case I would never see them again. "Yes," I lied. "That is my husband's handwriting."

THEY KEPT me at the hospital for a week. By that time, the police had finished their investigations in and around the house on the cliff. When the taxi dropped me off outside, in a blanket and borrowed hospital scrubs, I stood for a long time, staring up at the imposing facade.

The house looked different now, somehow. I didn't know how I felt about it anymore. I had no idea what I was going to do. With the house. With the rest of my life, that Anthony had gifted me through his actions. Part of me felt guilty and wanted to confess, just tell everyone the truth, but the rational part of my brain realized that even if I did, no one would have believed me. The evidence was clear, and no one doubted the scenario that Anthony had arranged after I fled from the house. An open and shut case, that's what they had said.

I let myself in with the keys that the police had dropped off at the hospital and wandered through the house, as if seeing it for the first time. The fridge was empty and the rooms were cold.

I would never be able to sell this house now, not with two deaths.

So, I guess I was stuck here.

I found a couple of tins in the cupboard and fixed

myself a makeshift dinner. Not until it began to get dark did I wander up the stairs to the second floor.

The door to the bedroom was open. I walked over and looked inside the room. It looked pretty much the same as before, but I knew that I would never sleep in there again. I couldn't even look at the bed without seeing Thomas's accusing stare. After I'd taken a shower and put on some proper clothes, I walked into the only finished guest room and crawled into bed there. Part of me was hoping that Anthony would show up and get into bed with me, just to hold me, but something told me that I had seen him for the last time. Getting me off the hook for killing Thomas had been his way of making good all the things that had gone wrong all those years ago, and hopefully, he'd been able to move on somehow.

I snuggled deeper under the covers and wondered what on earth I was supposed to do now.

3 4

I STAYED in the house on the cliff. I didn't have much of a choice in the matter since the realtor assured me that there was no way she would be able to sell the house now. The chances of another sucker like Thomas coming along and not being deterred by the fact that the last sucker had gone mad and killed himself after just a couple of months in the house were slim to not-ever-gonna-happen.

A lawyer sent me a letter, asking to see me. I drove myself into town, feeling like an alien come down to earth, all the perfectly normal things that went on around me so exotic, so alien. I went through the drive-through at a hamburger place and sat in the car, eating the biggest hamburger I had ever had, satisfying a craving that had been driving me mad lately. After being more or less vegetarian for years, I suddenly craved meat in any variety. And I was so hungry, all the time, constantly snacking.

The lawyer told me that since I was the only benefi-ciary, probate would just be a formality. The house was mine and all the assets. The numbers on the bank statements he placed before me made my jaw drop. I had thought that we were living hand to mouth, but apparently, Thomas had been keeping things from me. It was no fortune, but more than enough to keep the house warm and keep me in more of those giant hamburgers for a while, until I had figured things out.

After leaving the lawyer's office, I went shopping, filling the cart to the brim with everything that caught my eye.

As I was getting the bags out of the car back home, another car pulled up. Freddie got out and walked over to me.

"Hey, do you need a hand with that?"

I was going to tell him no, thanks, determined to keep my broken heart and my guilty conscience far away from him but then I figured that it was just a neighborly gesture and nothing more. And if I was going to stay on in a probably no longer haunted house, I could use a friendly neighbor. "Sure." I gave him a couple of the bags and walked ahead of him inside the house and to the kitchen.

He put the bags on the counter and started to unpack them, as if it was the most natural thing to do, even though he had barely set foot in this house before. My heart ached at how perfectly he fit in here, but I quenched the feeling. That was not the man for me. Not now. Not ever.

We chatted a little while I put the groceries away, about the weather and stuff, nothing important. I thought about my plans to throw myself out onto the dating scene and find a man who would want to have a child with me. With some money in the bank, I supposed I could have gone for the IVF on my own, but I didn't want that. I wanted this. A man by my side as I was unpacking the shopping, someone who handed me the stuff for the pantry and put the cereal on top of the fridge without asking if it went there.

The more we talked, the more it became painfully obvious that this guy, this lovely man, would have been perfect for me. We shared so many interests, had enjoyed many of the same books, dreamed of traveling to the same places—Machu Picchu, Rome, Tokyo—and just generally got along in a relaxed and groovy manner that I couldn't recall I'd ever had with any other man. There were just a couple of little details that tripped everything up. The fact that he was a cop and I had killed a man.

And the fact that he couldn't have any more children. He didn't even *want* any more children.

And I wanted a child so bad that I thought I would lose my mind over it.

WHEN HE LEFT, and I had locked the door behind him, I walked back out into the kitchen and started making myself a sandwich to soothe my sorrows with. Peanut butter and jelly and salami and pickles. Don't ask me why. It seemed like a good idea at the time. In the end, I made two large sandwiches and devoured them in no time. I'd better get started on that dating, because if this kept up, I was going to be too fat to attract the future father of my children.

AND SURE ENOUGH, a few weeks later I was putting on

my favorite pair of jeans one morning and discovered that I couldn't button them. There was no way. I cursed, pulled them back off and grabbed a pair of yoga pants instead, resolving to go for a walk later, to set up a regular exercise routine and get back in shape before things got really out of hand.

As I was fixing myself some breakfast, I felt a slight unease as I pulled the ingredients from the fridge. When I poured the coffee, I suddenly felt revolted by the smell, something that I usually loved. Sitting down at the table, I took one bite of my sandwich and felt my stomach turn.

I barely made it to the bathroom before the entire contents of my stomach—a whole bite of a sandwich and gallons of yellow bile—came pouring out of me and into the toilet bowl. I grabbed the sink with one hand and the wall with the other, just to keep on my feet. That was so strange. Stomach flu? I barely ever saw anyone that I could have caught it from, and I hadn't eaten anything yet today that could have gone off. If I had gotten food poisoning from something I ate yesterday, surely I would have noticed that during the night? I staggered back out to the kitchen but had to put everything away without eating another bite. I walked back upstairs to crawl into bed in the guest room which was my room now, but as I pulled the covers over me, a completely bizarre thought occurred to me.

No. That couldn't be. There was just no way. Impossible.

But still.

I hurried back downstairs, grabbed my coat and my car keys and got in the car, racing to the nearest drugstore. I searched the shelves until I found what I was looking for, hurried over to the counter and waited impatiently while the teller rang up my purchase.

Back in the car, I realized that I couldn't wait until I got back home, so I pulled into a gas station and ran inside to use their restroom.

The cubicle was narrow and the walls covered in graffiti, but I pulled open the box, fumbled open the instructions and then pulled my pants down, squatting over the stick.

Not a drop. I hadn't had anything to drink all day, and there was nothing coming out. I waited impatiently until I managed to squeeze out just a few drops. Then I pulled my yoga pants back up, walked back out to the car and sat in the driver's seat, staring at the dashboard clock. When the time was up, I picked up the stick and turned it over, staring at the little window.

I had expected it to be a blue line or maybe two, that was always how I had pictured this moment, but this was a more advanced variety of test or perhaps one that catered to rather stupid people who needed things spelled out for them. The word PREGNANT filled the small window. I still didn't get it. How could that be? It just couldn't. Thomas and I hadn't had sex in ages, and I knew for a fact that I'd had my regular period several times since we last …

Oh no.

Remember that love always triumphs over hate. Life over death.

Always, my lovely, always

Oh … no …?

Oh, Anthony. Yes!

WELL, even compared to all the other weird stuff that had been happening in my life lately, this really blew me away. In a good way, mostly. Perhaps not at first. But after I had been to the doctor's and had everything confirmed and she had told me that everything looked perfectly normal and fine and that there was no reason that I wouldn't have a healthy child despite the recent trauma, it slowly started to sink in. After ten years of being married and doing all the things that married people do without even so much as a false alarm, I had managed to get pregnant with a man that had been dead for decades. Talk about a potent manifestation!

The pregnancy progressed as normal as could be expected, with emotional and physical changes like a constant rollercoaster from day to day and sometimes hour to hour. Don't get me wrong. I was over the moon about the fact that I was pregnant. It was just the whole I-killed-my-husband, am-living-all-alone-in-a-haunted-house thing that sometimes got me a bit down in the dumps. I never saw a glimpse of Anthony again.

Not that I didn't try. I talked to him all the time, not sure if he could hear me, but I wanted him to know about the baby, about how I felt about what he had done for me. Both as regards to Thomas and the new life that was growing inside of me. Part of me—a big part—was kind of hoping that he would manifest again, that he could be here with me forever, like the perfect husband, forever young, forever handsome and with some pretty awesome skills in all kinds of areas. But I knew that wouldn't work. What kind of a mother would I be if I let my child grow up with a ghost for a father? Perhaps not something that you were bullied for in school, not for long anyway, but it might make it awkward and difficult to make friends.

No. Anthony wouldn't be a father to my child. It was just me. And as soon as I had gotten used to the idea, I dropped the whole dating plan as being just too weird. Who would want to date a pregnant woman, anyway?

Instead, I settled into some kind of routine. I got the rest of the house in order, with the help of some handymen from a couple of towns over who hadn't heard about the whole haunting thing. I went to auctions and found a nice antique store a bit further up the coast and started to furnish the rest of the house. After giving it a lot of thought, I completely redid the old master bedroom and transformed it into a bright and cheerful nursery, with a changing table where the writing desk had been, an old rocking chair where I could sit and look out over the ocean, soft rugs for learning to crawl, several shelves for books and toys and a beautiful antique swinging cot with a lace canopy instead of the big old bed where my baby most probably had been conceived.

The room looked completely transformed, and I didn't feel a hint of unease about the fact that this was the room where Thomas had died. I didn't even grieve for him much, and at first, I felt bad about that. After all, he was my husband, and my muddled memories from the night he died still made me wake up in the middle of the night, completely damp with sweat. But after a while, I realized that I had lost him many years ago when we had both fallen out of love and that I had grieved that loss and the demise of our marriage for many years before he actually passed away.

I had mostly managed to block out the traumatic events surrounding his death. I sometimes had nightmares and woke up gasping for air, certain that I could feel his arm pressing against my throat, but most of the time I managed to get back to sleep again by focusing on other memories, of lovemaking and comforting and even making a baby. That was what I wanted to remember from that night, not the horrible stuff.

I felt terribly guilty about what had happened, but slowly came to accept that it was just an unfortunate and completely unbelievable turn of events that had led to his death. I never meant to kill him, I never wanted to do him any kind of harm at all, not even when I found that lipstick on his collar. Grabbing that flashlight had been a reflex, I had just been trying to get him off me, to save my own life. It was just one of those random things that happened in life sometimes, a roll of the dice that ended unexpectedly. If I would have guessed how that night should have ended, it would have been me that had died, in all the different scenarios that I could think of. The fact that I was still alive had to mean something, there had to be a reason for me still being here, living and breathing, when Thomas was not. I had to cling to that belief, or I would go mad with guilt.

And this was not the time for guilt and regrets or for grief and sorrow, I thought, sitting in the rocking chair with one hand on the still empty cot and the other on my round stomach. This was the time to look toward the future. I spent many hours in that chair, picturing what it would be like, next year or the year after that. But in all my daydreams, there was always a blur at the edge of my vision, a part that was missing or incomplete. I could see my beautiful child and even see myself as a mother, as strange as it seemed. But there should be someone else. I knew that. I just had no idea where I could find him.

ONE SUNNY AFTERNOON at the beginning of June, my daydreaming was interrupted by a knock on the door. I walked down the stairs slowly, with a firm grip on the railing, and opened the door. Freddie was standing outside, surrounded by his children who were clearly excited about something.

"We'we going on a picnic," exclaimed Bridget before Freddie had a chance to speak. "And you awe coming with us."

I looked at her and then at her father. "Oh?" I said. "I don't think …"

"Oh, please say you'll come," said Freddie. "My parents are away on a cruise, and I've been stuck with the kids all alone the entire Easter. If I don't get to speak to an adult soon, I'll most definitely go mad."

I couldn't help but smile at him. I couldn't remember when I had last had a proper conversation with another person, adult or child. That must mean that I was already stark raving mad. Come to think of it, I was walking around this big empty house, talking to a ghost and to my unborn child all day. "All right then," I said. "Let me just get my coat."

"You don't need one," Timmy said confidently. I could definitely see traces of Freddie in the boy. "It's really warm outside."

I grabbed my coat just in case and pulled it on before waddling along with them through the meadow and through the trees on the other side. It was slow going, but Freddie didn't seem to mind the pace and the children were running around and exploring all over anyway, so it wasn't as if I was slowing them down.

"Not far to go now?" Freddie asked and looked at my stomach which protruded rather obviously from within my coat.

"Oh, six or seven weeks," I said and put my hand on the top of the swelling where I had just felt a kick.

I could see him doing the math, but he didn't say anything. We kept walking, and it was a lovely day. The sun was shining, and the children had soon shed their coats. We didn't go far, just over to the trees on the other side of the fence so that we wouldn't be assaulted by ferocious cows on the prowl. Freddie had a big blanket that he spread out on the grass, and I sank gratefully down on it, loosening my shoelaces. It had been ages since I had walked that far and my feet felt terribly swollen.

Freddie unpacked the hamper, mostly cookies and store-bought treats, but the kids didn't mind. They were soon up and running again, only doing short pit stops to get a drink or grab a cookie. I watched them with fascination and listened intently to the very intricate backstory they made up for the game they devised. Soon they were busy trying to reclaim the treasure (an empty juice carton some previous visitor had left behind) from the vicious Trellari (a couple of unsuspecting cows on the other side of the fence) with the use of a long stick. I leaned back and watched them play. It was amazing how they could create entire worlds and characters like that, out of nothing more than some pieces of trash and their limitless imaginations.

Freddie lay back and closed his eyes for a while, and I couldn't help but look at him. The soft curls still enticed my fingers to reach for them and his almost constantly smiling lips looked so very kissable. He had stopped by now and then, offering to help me around the house, and even though I had tried my best to keep the distance, I had found myself accepting his offers more and more as my stomach had grown over the past few months and for less and less cumbersome tasks, such as opening the pickle jar or getting something down from the top shelf after I became afraid of getting up on a chair. Afraid of falling or afraid of breaking the chair with my rather impressive weight, I won't say. I really enjoyed his company, but it was obvious that he considered me a friend and nothing more. Perhaps not even that. An acquaintance, maybe.

But he had taken to spending regular weekends with the kids at his parents' house, and I wasn't entirely sure that it was just because the children loved it out here. In fact, Timmy had told me several times that he preferred his dad's apartment in town, because of its proximity to the pizza place downstairs and all the video games in his dad's vast collection. And he had invited me to this lovely picnic.

I turned and looked out over the sea, worried that I might bend over and kiss him if I kept staring at those delectable lips much longer. The blue sky from an hour ago was rapidly shrinking, due to heavy dark clouds that were moving in toward the coastline. Slanted streaks of rain hung like a curtain down to the water. I reached out and put my hand on Freddie's arm to wake him. But before I had the chance to say anything, he lifted his own hand and placed it on top of mine. It was such a small gesture, but so intensely affectionate that I felt a pinch in my heart. No, not merely an acquaintance.

"I think we ought to go back," I said softly, not wanting to break the spell.

He opened one eye, looked at me and then up at the sky. As soon as he saw the clouds, he sat up and called out to the children to come and get their coats. He quickly gathered all the trash in the hamper and helped me up before folding the blanket. We had only just begun walking back when the clouds pulled in over land, and it started to rain. I walked as fast as I could, but that was not very fast, and soon the rain was pelting down.

"You should go," I yelled at Freddie when he put an arm around me to help me keep my balance on the muddy path. "You and the kids are getting soaked. Run back to the car; you don't have to wait for me. I'll get home eventually."

He just stared at me. "I'm not leaving you out here," he said, as if I had suggested something entirely preposterous. "Oh, no."

Slowly, we made it back to the house, and I staggered up on the porch where the children who had run ahead where huddled out of the rain. "Well, thank you for a lovely picnic," I said and smiled at them, my teeth chattering from the cold. "Hurry on home now, before you all catch colds."

My fingers were cold and stiff, and I fumbled with getting the key in the lock. Freddie took them from me and unlocked the door. "No, we'd better go in with you," he said. "Make sure you're all right." He looked worried, and I couldn't for the life of me understand why until I stepped inside the door and caught a glimpse of myself in the mirror on the wall by the hall closet. I was pale as a ghost, and my lips were blue. Every step I took showed on my face as a twinge of pain from my ankles that had swollen to twice their normal size.

"I'm fine," I assured him. "I just need to run a bath to get warm again. Don't worry about me." I turned and looked at the children. "You need to worry about *them.*"

Freddie glanced at his kids. "Are you all right?" he asked and got three nodding heads in response. "Well, can you three play nice while I help Lisa?" The heads nodded again. "All right then. Is it okay if they explore or are there any rooms in the house where you don't want them to go?"

I shook my head. "No, they can go wherever they want."

"No fragile collectibles or a room furnished entirely with furniture made out of china?"

"Well, if you do go in the china room, please don't sit on anything," I told the children as Freddie led me toward the stairs. "Other than that, feel free to roam."

Freddie took me upstairs and turned on the taps for me as I sat on the closed toilet lid, trying to unbutton my coat with numb fingers. Freddie bent down and did it for me and then proceeded to remove my shoes and the rest of my clothes until he reached for my maternity dress and I had to stop him.

"No," I said softly. "That's all right. I can manage from here."

He immediately backed away. "Of course. I'll be right outside. Holler if you need me."

He was halfway out the door when the words slipped out under my breath. "Trust me; you do *not* want to see that."

He stopped with his hand on the door handle and turned toward me. "Trust *me*; you look absolutely beautiful." Then he smiled, stepped out into the hallway and closed the door behind him.

I HAVE no idea how I managed to get into that bathtub, but after a good long soak I felt much better. As I walked back to the bedroom to get dressed, I heard voices from the nursery. When I came back out into the hallway a little while later, with a thick knitted cardigan over my maternity sweats and knitted socks on my swollen feet, I could only hear one. Freddie's.

I moved over to the door, and when I looked in, I saw him sitting in the rocker, with Bridget on his lap and the boys sitting on the soft rug in front. He was reading from one of the books I had bought, a favorite of mine from when I was little, and the children were transfixed. I stood there for a long while, just taking in the beautiful scene in front of me. Freddie's voice was soft and melodious, and when he read the final scene in the book, where the rabbit finds its way back home again, I felt tears welling up in my eyes.

He closed the book, kissed Bridget on the forehead and looked at the boys. "I used to read that book to you when you were little, do you remember?"

Timmy nodded, having probably heard the story when his younger siblings were small as well, but Bridget and Zach shook their heads. Bridget's cheeks were all flushed. "Did I cwy, daddy?" she asked. "Did I cwy when you wead that book? I think I did, when I was a baby." I could see her pulling herself up and trying to distance herself from that time.

"I still cry every time I hear that story," I said and stepped inside the room.

Everyone turned toward me, and I just wanted to grab them and hug them, all of them. They looked so perfect sitting there, as if they belonged, and I realized with a pang that this was what I had been missing. The whole family. Just me and the baby wouldn't be the same.

"How was your bath?" asked Freddie.

"Fine. I'm feeling much better. How about you? Are you cold? I could make some cocoa," I suggested.

The kids erupted in enthusiastic whoops but Freddie shook his head. "You need to stay off your feet. I'll make the cocoa. And you play nice," he said to the kids. "I'll call you when it's done."

The children nodded eagerly and continued to explore the contents of the shelves.

Freddie offered me his arm on the way down the stairs, and I took it gratefully. He was probably right about me staying off my feet. They were still swollen and throbbed a little.

Out in the kitchen, he pulled out a chair for me, and I sat down slowly. He pulled out another chair and put my feet up on it. "Better?"

"Much. Thank you."

"Oh, it's my pleasure." He started moving around the

kitchen, finding most of what he needed and me pointing out the rest. Soon there was a large pot of sweet cocoa simmering on the stove, and he called the children downstairs. They came like thunder down the stairs, and stormed out into the kitchen, looking around them at everything new.

"You sure have many rooms here," Zach commented when he was sitting at the table with a big mug of cocoa in front of him. "Do you really live here all alone?"

I nodded. Then I put my hand on my stomach and smiled. "But not for long."

"But that's just a little baby," Zach complained. "I know what room the baby is going to live in. But you have so many other rooms that don't even have any furniture in them. Who's going to live there?"

I shrugged. "I don't know. Maybe no one. Maybe I'll turn one room into a sewing room, and one room into a reading room, and one room into a ..." I tried to think.

"... a Lego room!" said Timmy enthusiastically.

"... a doll's woom!" said Bridget longingly.

"... a candy room!" said Zach but then his smile vanished. "But really, it's not fair. I don't even have my own room at Dad's. I have to share with Timmy." He turned toward his dad. "I wish you had a big house like this so that I could have my own room."

Freddie put his hand on his shoulder and gave his son an apologetic smile. "I wish I had a big house like this, too," he said. "In fact, when I was your age, I used to dream about living in this house."

They disappeared into a conversation about what Freddie had been like as a child and what it had been like living with Grandma and Grandpa all the time, but I didn't hear much of what was said. My head was filled with a whole new daydream, a perfect one, where they all lived here with me and everyone got their own room except for Freddie who would share mine and then I started thinking about what it would be like to share a room with Freddie and crawl into bed with him at night, and it had been such a long time since I had even thought about something like that that my body didn't know what to do with itself. I took another sip of the cocoa and hoped that my blushing cheeks would be blamed on the cold that I would surely come down with after this adventure.

When all the cocoa was gone, the kids disappeared for some more exploring and Freddie got up and started doing the dishes, despite my protests.

"I mean it," he said. "You need to keep off your feet. You must take care of yourself now. And the little one."

"I know." I sighed. This part was definitely missing from this pregnancy. The husband who helped out and cared and comforted and … and loved me. I sighed again and felt an intense sadness come over me. Oh, this baby was a dream come true, but it turns out that I had more than one dream.

When Freddie was done, I started to get up to follow them to the door, but the baby kicked so violently that I stopped halfway up and gave out a little yelp.

Freddie turned toward me. "What is it?"

I grabbed the table and pulled myself the rest of the way up. "Nothing. Just my little Maradona in here, practicing his penalty kicks on some vital organ."

His face lit up. "The baby is kicking? Oh, can I feel?"

I nodded and he hurried over, putting both hands on my stomach. "Where?"

I almost couldn't breathe with him standing so

close to me, but I took one of his hands and moved it to the place where the last kick had landed. The baby immediately kicked again, right into Freddie's hand. "Oh!" he whispered. "Wow!" His hands were moving over my round stomach in search of the next assault. Another kick and I could see that he had felt it too. "Amazing," he whispered. He raised his head and looked me straight into the eyes. He was so close; I could almost feel his breath on my face. His smile was so radiant and his eyes so very blue, I couldn't stop staring at them. There were these small lines in the corners of his eyes, and it was the most adorable thing I had ever seen. I had to restrain myself to not reach out and caress them or even plant a featherlight kiss there.

Oh, my goodness, he stood so very close. And his hands were so very soft against my stomach. And he smelled so sweet, like cocoa and rain and … Oh, my.

One of his hands wandered up to the top of my stomach, resting on it, just underneath my full breast. He kept staring at me, and I couldn't take my eyes off him when he slipped his hand inside my cardigan and up under my sweatshirt. His hand was soft and warm against my stretched skin, and when the baby kicked straight at his hand again, it felt like the most intimate experience of my life. I hadn't thought that I would ever feel anything remotely sexual again, not after all the weirdness that had been going on with my body the last few months, but if the children hadn't come down the stairs at that very moment, I don't know what I would have done.

Freddie slowly leaned closer and gave me the lightest kiss on the lips, before pulling slowly and with apparent reluctance back again. "Amazing," he whispered again. "Thank you."

"No, thank *you*," I croaked, not being able to put enough words together to make a longer sentence than that.

The kids stormed out into the kitchen again, and Freddie told them to go put on their jackets. Once they had disappeared out the door again, he turned toward me.

"My parents get back from their cruise tonight," he murmured. "I could come by later." He paused for a moment before continuing. "Just to make sure that you are all right."

Oh, he could make everything all right, I didn't doubt that for a minute. "Okay," I whispered.

I stood in the hallway watching them drive off, trying to rein in my emotions and all my physical urges. Perhaps this wasn't such a good idea. Perhaps this wasn't the best time. Perhaps.

But I knew that if he returned, there would be no holding me back.

As the evening progressed, I started to come to my senses. Of course, he hadn't meant anything like what I had imagined. Who gives a very pregnant woman a booty call? No one. I didn't want any man to see me like this, and especially not that man, the perfect man, the one I had all these daydreams about. He would just take one look at my veiny breasts and thick ankles and remember that he'd left the stove on or something. Stupid. This was just what happened when a woman was widowed too young. She had urges that when left unmet could drive her to assault poor polite neighbors who didn't realize how very delectable their full lips were.

I wished that I could have a glass of wine to calm my nerves. Instead, I had a cup of tea, and it had no effect on my urges at all. Typical.

When I heard the knock on the door, I almost didn't answer it. But then I did. Of course, I did.

He stood outside, not with an eager grin on his face but rather an apologetic smile. Of course. He had already remembered about the stove being on. He had just come to say that he wouldn't be coming. I knew it.

"I'm sorry," he began, and I simultaneously died inside and sighed with relief. "Perhaps this wasn't such a good idea."

"Perhaps not," I said.

"It's just …" He looked at me. "Can I come in?"

I stepped to the side and let him in. We walked into the living room and sat down on the sofa at a polite distance. I didn't understand why he had to come in to say that he didn't want to be here, but here we were.

"I know this isn't the best time," he began. "With you …" He nodded at my stomach. "And me being divorced less than a year." He sighed and leaned back. "They say you should wait a year after a divorce or a bereavement before you make any big life decisions. Before you take on the commitment of a new relationship."

"I understand," I mumbled. And really, I did. But even though my brain was totally on board with his reasoning, the rest of my body was not listening.

"Do you?" He sounded sad.

"Sure."

I couldn't look at him, had to force my eyes in another direction, because I didn't want to see the relief in his eyes when he realized that he was off the hook. That he wouldn't be expected to get it up for the beached whale at the other end of the sofa.

But then he moved closer. "But do you?" he asked and took my hand. I had to look at him then. There was no getting away from it.

He looked sad. He looked confused. He looked … oh my, he looked almost as desperate as I felt. "Yeah," I said. "You don't want to do this. I totally understand. I'm a big girl. Literally. I can take it. It's fine. You can go. I'll see you around sometime."

He shook his head. "Oh, no. I so want to do this. I can't think of anything else. Nothing but you. But not just this, not just …" He reached out and kissed me again, and at the same time he put his hand on my swollen breast and caressed it slowly while his thumb rubbed over my nipple that was pressing against the fabric. He pulled back just a little from my mouth. "Not just this, even though this is very much on my mind just now. But I'm afraid that I'm getting ahead of myself. Because I can't stop thinking about you and me, and you and me and the baby, and you and me and the baby and the kids and about Christmas here and all the birthdays and all the summer holidays and where I'm going to hide the eggs for the Easter hunt and how we're going to grow old here, you and me, and how the kids are going to come and visit with their families and all the grandchildren running around the house and …" He sighed. "And I know that it is too soon to be thinking about anything like that. I have barely even kissed you yet." He kissed me again, just to prove a point. "But oh, Lisa … Don't ever think that I don't want this," another flick of the thumb and my nipple was almost forcing its way out through both bra and sweatshirt by now. "Don't ever think that I wouldn't throw myself at you and ravage you senseless, given the slightest hint of encouragement."

I gasped for air. I didn't know what turned me on more, his skilled fingers moving over my body or his plans for our retirement. But turned on, I was.

"Encouragement?" I said, breathlessly. "You mean like: Go, Freddie," I whispered. "Or: You can do it!"

He moaned and dove down between my breasts, tugging at any piece of fabric that came in his way. "Yes," he said while licking my skin and shifting me on the sofa so that he could reach every part of me better. "Exactly like that."

He pulled off my sweat pants and kissed my leg all the way from my knitted socks up to the inside of my thigh. Then he buried his face in my soft folds and went from acquaintance to lover in less than 60 seconds. "Freddie, Freddie, he's our man," I moaned and wriggled beneath him. "If he can't do it, no one can …"

He laughed and moved up along my body, kissing every bit of naked skin he came across on the way. "Oh, I think I can," he said and unbuckled his belt, proving to anyone who might be watching that he, in fact, could, yes, indeed. He pulled my bottom out onto the edge of the sofa and pushed inside of me while standing on his knees on the floor so as to not put any weight on my stomach. "I think I can …" he said over and over and plunged repeatedly deep inside me, gripping my hips hard and locking eyes with me the whole time.

I came first, so hard that I almost blacked out and was worried for a moment when my stomach went rock hard, but Freddie assured me that it was normal and that the baby wouldn't be harmed by this. Then he kept moving inside of me, caressing my breasts, telling me over and over how wonderful I was, how good I felt, how much he wanted me. He pulled one of my legs up onto his shoulder and started pushing faster and harder at the same time as he caressed the hard nodule at the top of my soft folds. I didn't think that I could come again so soon, but before long I felt the familiar surge again and grabbed his arm and adjusted his rhythm to what I needed at the moment. When he was starting to look strained, I grabbed his hand, took one of his fingers in my mouth and sucked as hard as I could. The climax was simultaneous and intense, and his convulsions inside of me only enhanced my pleasure.

He climbed up next to me on the sofa and pulled a rug over us both, kissing the side of my neck as he snuggled up behind me. "What do you think?" he asked softly. "Would you like to … I don't know, go out on a date or something?"

I shook my head. "No," I replied. "I think you should just move in."

If there was one thing that I had learned, it was that life is short. And I didn't want to waste another minute of it on being lonely.

He put his arms around me and caressed my stomach.

"Are you sure that you're up for it?" I asked gently. "I thought that you didn't want any more children."

He sat up. "When have I ever said that?"

"You said that three was a good number," I reminded him.

He lay back down behind me, pulling me closer. "Four is an even better number in many ways," he said. Then he paused for a minute. "If you ask me, five is a great number, for that matter. And six, well, that is an even half-dozen, which is good in so many ways."

I felt a wave of relief surging up through my body. This might feel like it was too good to be true, but I figured I was owed a decade or so of absolute euphoria after the last ten years.

I had read somewhere that vasectomies could be reversed. And if it couldn't, there was always adoption.

Thanks to Anthony, I'd gotten the chance to experience a pregnancy, and I would soon have a baby of my very own. But I knew deep down that Freddie was the love of my life and that his children would be a natural part of my family. He was my happily ever after. And I couldn't wait to spend the rest of eternity with him.

As someone once wrote to me; always, my lovely, always.

THE END

Award-winning journalist Susan Armstrong always gets her story. Seven months pregnant, she receives some very disturbing news and flies halfway around the world to find a former interview victim that might be the only person in the world that can help her. If he is willing to break a few laws, both legal and moral, for a woman he only met briefly, ten years ago, that is. And fast, because time is ticking and Susan is up against a completely new kind of deadline. Perhaps even a literal one?